Jailbird Kid

ALSO BY SHIRLEE SMITH MATHESON

NONFICTION

Youngblood of the Peace

This Was Our Valley

Flying the Frontiers Volume I:
A Half-Million Hours of Aviation Adventure

Flying the Frontiers Volume II:
More Hours of Aviation Adventure

Flying the Frontiers Volume III:
Aviation Adventures Around the World

A Western Welcome to the World:
The History of Calgary International Airport

Lost: True Stories of Canadian Aviation Tragedies

Maverick in the Sky:
The Aerial Adventures of WWI Flying Ace Freddie McCall

Amazing Flights and Flyers

TEEN FICTION

Prairie Pictures

City Pictures

Flying Ghosts

The Gambler's Daughter

Keeper of the Mountains

Fastback Beach

Jailbird Kid

Shirlee Smith Matheson

DUNDURN PRESS

TORONTO

Editor: Michael Carroll

Design: Jennifer Scott
Printer: Webcom

Library and Archives Canada Cataloguing in Publication

Matheson, Shirlee Smith
        Jailbird kid / by Shirlee Smith Matheson.

ISBN 978-1-55488-704-0

        I. Title.

PS8576.A823J34 2010   jC813'.54   C2009-907473-7

1   2   3   4   5   14   13   12   11   10

  Conseil des Arts   Canada Council   Canadä   ONTARIO ARTS COUNCIL
                       du Canada   for the Arts   CONSEIL DES ARTS DE L'ONTARIO

We acknowledge the support of the **Canada Council for the Arts** and the **Ontario Arts Council** for our publishing program. We also acknowledge the financial support of the **Government of Canada** through the **Canada Book Fund** and **The Association for the Export of Canadian Books**, and the **Government of Ontario** through the **Ontario Book Publishers Tax Credit program**, and the **Ontario Media Development Corporation**.

Care has been taken to trace the ownership of copyright material used in this book. The author and the publisher welcome any information enabling them to rectify any references or credits in subsequent editions.

                                        J. Kirk Howard, President

Printed and bound in Canada.
www.dundurn.com

        Dundurn Press   Gazelle Book Services Limited   Dundurn Press
    3 Church Street, Suite 500   White Cross Mills   2250 Military Road
    Toronto, Ontario, Canada   High Town, Lancaster, England   Tonawanda, NY
          M5E 1M2   LA1 4XS   U.S.A. 14150

 Mixed Sources
Product group from well-managed forests, controlled sources and recycled wood or fiber
www.fsc.org Cert no. SW-COC-002358
© 1996 Forest Stewardship Council
FSC

 **ANCIENT FOREST** ™
FRIENDLY

To Devon. And to families like Angela's:
Per ardua ad astra —
"through adversity to the stars."

1
Birds

Today at school our grade nine teacher, Mrs. Madsen, made me stand on my desk while everyone sang "Happy Birthday." I hated it. I didn't want people to notice me.

I looked over at my friend, Ryan Phelps, and he gave me a high-five.

Ryan was crazy about computers and always put in extra time in the computer lab. He had a powerful computer at home, too, with a million games on it. He, Hannah Singer, and I were always on Instant Messenger, which was easier than phoning because we could all talk at once. When Ryan was online, he was "Judge Dredd." Hannah was "Perfect Pliés," since she was totally into ballet; she'd been doing it for years. I came on as "B-Phlat," as in a music note — not my body, please! My mom, who once played in a country music band, was teaching me to play the guitar. I'd had enough sorrow and heartbreak and crazy stuff in my life already to write a hundred country songs.

My friends and I were all really different, but it was just us three that hung together. Ryan was tall and skinny and wore what he felt most comfortable in, usually a hoodie and jeans. Hannah was quite beautiful and dressed very smart. And me, I was sort of in the middle — mostly casual, but I liked to look nice, too. That came from my mom. She was very classy.

But, in fact, I told *nobody* here about my "private life," not even Ryan or Hannah — especially Hannah because her dad was a bank manager and, well, my private story just wouldn't go over very well if she told her parents.

"Why aren't you having a birthday party, Angela?" Hannah asked me at the fifteen-minute break between classes.

"Oh, Mom's too busy. She's been working long hours. I'll have a party later, maybe in the summer holidays."

"Sounds great."

Hannah gave me a cool present — a beautiful necklace with little bird charms made from jewels and tumbled rocks. Hannah's mom was an artist. She made all sorts of jewellery — bracelets and rings and things like this cool necklace.

Hannah became my first friend when Mom and I moved from our too-small hometown into this small but bigger city when I was in grade seven. When we came here and rented our little house, I made up a story. Okay, a lie. I said my dad was working out of town and wasn't home much.

The truth was, my dad's release date from prison, and my fifteenth birthday, fall on the same day: June 5.

There was no way I could have a birthday party. What would I do if my friends and I were playing games and Dad walked in? What would he be like after two years? I'd have to stop everything, say "Hi!" as if he'd just been out for a walk, and introduce him to my friends. "Hey, this is my dad. He just got out of jail."

The day of my birthday was so hot you could fry eggs on the sidewalk. I walked home from school, wearing my new necklace and carrying a book my teacher had given me: *Bedtime Ghost Stories for Young People*. Yeah, right, just the thing to chase away my nightmares. I also had Ryan's present, a science fantasy book called *Space-Song*, featuring my favourite character, Princess Anya. I was thinking that maybe Mom would order in a pizza or Chinese food to celebrate my birthday, or we might go out.

I came around the corner and stopped dead in my tracks. All plans vanished. My dusty front lawn looked like a hostel for street people. In fact, it was Grandma Wroboski, Aunt Gemma, my dad's younger sister who was eighteen, and two men. Plus bags of groceries loaded onto the front steps and porch. I stopped before they saw me.

Gemma was lounging on the lawn with her shirt rolled up, likely trying to get a tan. Her silver belly-button ring gleamed in the sun. Grandma had sunk into a rickety lawn chair she'd found somewhere. She was wearing a pink-flowered summer dress that shrouded her big body like a tent, and wide plastic flip-flops decorated with white daisies. Grandma was fanning her face with a magazine and sipping a can of pop. The men were squatting in the shade, smoking. One had his shirt off, revealing his tattoo-covered chest and arms, and the other was wearing a white T-shirt with the sleeves ripped off.

When Gemma rolled onto her stomach, she spotted me and waved lazily. "Hi, Angela! We've been waiting for you. Happy birthday, kid!" She flicked her fuchsia fingernails at me. I noticed the colour matched her toe-nails and her newly highlighted blond hair.

Grandma tried to heave herself out of the lawn chair, but it remained suctioned to her bum. When she

stood, hunched over, she was still wearing it. One of
the men held the chair while the other jumped up to
give her a hand.

"Hot, hot, hot," Grandma said, panting. "Lord love
a duck, it's supposed to be over thirty degrees today."
She held out her big brown arms and sailed toward me.
"My little angel! Fifteen years old! All grown up!"

I ran to give her a hug. She smelled like ginger.

"We brought stuff to make a birthday supper for you
and a homecoming supper for your daddy," Gemma
said, indicating the bags on the porch. "If we don't get
these chickens into the fridge, they're going to come to
life again and start squawking."

I stared at the men.

"This here's Mike, and this is Jerry," Gemma said.
"Maybe you remember them. Friends of mine and your
daddy's. They've come to say hi."

I knew who they were — guys that Mom called "the
outlaws." Like my dad, they'd do anything for the boss,
our Uncle Al. And, like my dad, they got into lots of
trouble because of it.

Grandma and Gemma hoisted some of the bags off
the porch and waited for me to unlock the door. The
men carried in more bags, cases of pop, and other stuff
they'd brought.

Amid the clanging and muttering, Grandma stopped

and put her hand to her ear. "Listen!" I couldn't hear a thing, but we stopped our noise and there it was — a sound like a tiny motorboat flip-flapping in the water. It came again.

Grandma dropped her bags and waddled back to a half-filled rain barrel at the corner of the house. She leaned over until her head was inside the barrel and her round pink-flowered bottom was balanced precariously on the barrel's edge. "Well, look at this, will you!" her voice boomed from inside the barrel. Her arms moved down and around as if attempting to scoop something out.

Gemma and I got closer. Grandma surfaced, and in her hand was a young robin, its feathers a dark slick.

"It's dead!" I cried.

But Grandma didn't listen. She pried open the tiny beak with her thumb and finger, put her mouth over it, and blew. Again and again, *puff, puff.* Then she massaged its tiny chest and back with her fingers, holding the limp little body gently in her hands.

The bird shuddered, its breast fluttering as it began to throb. Grandma grinned. "Poor little twerp. Just about a goner."

She wiped the bird dry using the folds of her dress. When the ruffled feathers were filled with air, she set it on the grass. The bird struggled to its feet.

"He'll be okay in a couple of minutes, as long as a cat don't see him. You girls keep watch. It's too doggone hot out here for me."

Grandma picked up a couple of bags and went inside the house, leaving Gemma and me to bird-sit. It hopped along the grass, stopped for a rest, and tried its wings. We lifted it into a bush where it flapped from one branch to another.

"Looks like it'll live," Gemma said, snapping her gum.

Grandma appeared in the doorway, happily watching the bird hop to higher branches. "That little fella reminds me of your daddy," she said softly. "Some of God's creatures just need a little push."

We went inside. The house was hot, quiet, and full of flies. We couldn't keep them out if we wanted the windows open, since we didn't have screens. Mom didn't like spraying with chemicals, so we put up with the flies.

But Grandma had her own method of getting rid of them. She heated a long knife on the stove burner and held it up against a piece of yellow stuff that smelled like cough medicine. The flies took one sniff and were gone.

"Camphor," Grandma announced triumphantly. "Old pioneer trick. I got lots more, too. Now, Angela, where does your mamma keep her deep fryer? We got enough chicken here to feed an army."

So that was how all those birds came into my life on my birthday: Grandma's chickens, which were the best-tasting in the world; my new necklace; and a half-drowned baby robin. And, of course, there was "the famous jail-bird," as Gemma once called my dad, expected home any minute from a long "business trip" out of town.

2
In-Laws/Outlaws

We were peeling potatoes and hard-boiled eggs for a salad when Mom arrived from her receptionist job in a downtown office.

"Connie, honey, you go and change out of that hot outfit and pantyhose into something cool," Grandma said to Mom. "We've brought stuff for Angela's birthday and Nick's homecoming."

"You remember Mike and Jerry?" Gemma asked, nodding toward them.

Mike, who was standing by the door, threw his cigarette butt out onto the sidewalk and extended his hand toward Mom. She ignored it and brushed past him. I thought about how easily a fire could start on this hot day on the dry lawn, so I went out to stomp on the butt with my shoe, then bent to pick it up.

"Let me," Mike said.

"Don't!" Mom signalled for me to go inside, then glared at Mike. "You and your friend — just *get*!"

We all stood there, shocked.

"Wh-what?" Mike sputtered.

"You heard me. Leave my house. Both of you. I want you out of here." She nodded toward Jerry, who was standing with his arm casually draped around Gemma's shoulders.

"Hey, just a minute!" Jerry said. "We came to see our old pal, the Weasel. And to wish the kid a happy birthday."

Mom cringed, hearing the gross nickname they called my dad, but stood her ground. "Well, you've said happy birthday, now go."

I knew there was going to be a fight, like the kind I used to hear. I slammed into the house past Grandma, who had her back to them sorting groceries at the kitchen counter, and went to my bedroom, but not before I heard something I wished I hadn't. It was Mike's voice, gone hard and cold.

"C'mon, Con, you don't need to get uppity with old friends."

I heard the front door slam, Jerry mumbling something, and Gemma crying, "Hey, *you* don't hafta ..." And then the men were gone.

Mom entered my bedroom. "When did *they* get here?" She was really angry.

"They were waiting on the lawn."

"Oh, great. All the neighbours likely saw."

"Mom, they're dad's friends, and Gemma and Grandma are our relatives! We can't hide them now that Dad's coming home."

"Grandma and Gemma are okay, but not those two traitors." Mom sighed and wriggled her feet out of her shoes. "I'd planned to take you out for supper as a birthday treat," she said, stroking her feet, "but I guess we can celebrate at home tonight." I could tell she was thinking about Dad, and the homecoming of the "in-laws and outlaws," as she called his family and friends.

"It'll be okay, won't it, Mom?" I asked. I'd had dreams about Dad's homecoming, too, some good and some not so good. In fact, I'd thought about nothing else for the past few weeks.

She sighed deeply again. "Angel, I'm frankly quite concerned. I haven't seen your dad for two years. People change. It's like I heard about marriages that happened during the war. Some couples met and married within a few weeks or days. Then the men would be sent overseas. When they came back, nobody recognized each other. They had to wear name tags at their homecoming."

"But Dad wrote letters to us ..."

Mom laughed. "If you can call them that."

Dad's letters, especially to Mom, *were* kind of strange. The censors at the prison had blackened or cut out places where he apparently talked about crime or his fellow inmates, or swore. Some of his letters contained more holes than news.

But his letters to me weren't like that. "I love you and miss you," he'd write. "This is what I look like now." He'd draw a clown with big tears rolling down his cheeks. Even the flower in his hat was wilted. "But here's what I'll look like when I see you again." Same clown, but the flower on his hat stood straight up, his eyes smiled, and a happy grin stretched from ear to ear.

Dad was a good artist, but most of his pictures were weird, like the last one he sent. It was done in blue pastel crayons and showed two little monsters crawling out of a graveyard. He titled it *Two Little Ghouls in Blue*.

"Well, honey, we'll just have to make the best of it," Mom said. She stood and opened the door, heading for the shower. "Happy birthday, by the way. Your present's being delivered tomorrow. I think you'll like it."

I joined Grandma and Gemma in the kitchen. They were telling stories about Dad when he was little. I sat down to listen.

"Nicky always seemed to be in the right place at the

wrong time," Grandma was saying, "and then he got blamed for other people's dirty work. Like that terrible time when he got four years in the pen for armed robbery. Not his fault! When the police brought him in to answer those cooked-up charges, they just *ruined* his career with the horse-racing track."

"He was on the Ten Most Wanted list before they found him!" Gemma said proudly.

"Gemma, that's your big imagination running away with you! Nicky was never on that list. That's for serious criminals! Nicky's just unlucky. He's not serious at all." Grandma stopped for a drink of cream soda. "The best thing that ever happened to him was when he got out of the penitentiary, came home, and met Connie."

"So, see, it turned into a good thing, after all!" Gemma said.

Grandma shot her a disgusted look. "He didn't meet her *there*, in that prison. He met her in his own home, which he should never have left in the first place!"

Gemma liked to talk about crime stuff. She read *True Detective* and *Real Crime* and all those magazines, hoping she'd see someone she knew. She cut out every article about that old criminal Al Capone — Dad's and Uncle Al's big hero — and pasted them in a scrapbook. And then she cut out pictures of *her* hero, Jesse James. She freaked when I told her I'd learned on the Net that they were going to dig up his old grave and do a DNA test on his bones.

One year she framed Dad's police mug shot and gave it to Grandma for Christmas. Grandma didn't like it, though. She put a horse picture in the frame instead.

When we lived in our old town, we spent a lot of time with Grandma and her husband, Hank, especially after Mom's parents moved down to California. I called him Grandpa Hank, and he was nice. They got married the year before I was born. I never knew Grandpa Wroboski. "Hank's a *good man*," Grandma always said. "Unlike *some* people I could name."

I knew who she was referring to. Grandma despised Uncle Al, who was Grandpa Wroboski's brother. "That man never did anyone a speck of good," Grandma would say, when Uncle Al's name was mentioned. "He gets everyone into trouble except himself. Poor Nicky would never have gone to jail, not even once, if it wasn't for Al interfering in his life."

Mom came back into the kitchen, fresh from her shower and dressed in a T-shirt and shorts. Her long dark hair was pulled back into a ponytail. She was really pretty and only thirty-one years old.

"You look nice," Grandma said. "Nicky's sure gonna be happy to see you and Angela. It's good for both of you that he's coming home. Angela's getting to an age when she wants her daddy."

"What are you cooking?" Mom asked, snapping the tab off a can of Coke. She threw some ice cubes into two glasses and poured a drink for each of us. Grandma already had her favourite, cherry cream soda, and Gemma opened a beer.

"We brought some chickens and we've got the makings for potato salad," Gemma said. "Thought we could have a party for Nick."

Mom said nothing, but her lips compressed into a tight line. I knew she didn't want a party for Dad. She didn't want his homecoming to be advertised.

"Mix up that stuff for the salads, Gemma," Grandma ordered, then eased back into her chair.

I got up to help.

"We'll get this show on the road and then I'll give you the present I brought you," Gemma said to me with a secret smile.

I wondered what it would be. Probably something Mom wouldn't like. Mom said that Gemma was "eighteen going on twenty-five." She wore too much makeup, and her blond hair had a kind of purplish neon glow from so many perms and colour experiments. I liked her, though. She might have looked kind of tough, but she was always nice to me and fun to have around.

You never knew what was going to happen with Gemma. She'd finished grade twelve and started working immediately in a big department store downtown. Gemma was hoping to become the cosmetics and beauty department manager someday.

"That Nicky! I'll never forget when he was a kid." Grandma's face had lost its redness, and she sat back, relaxed. "The other kids would be out playing road hockey, and Nicky, he'd be inside. 'Anything I can do for you, Mamma?' he'd say. 'Shovel snow? Split wood? Anything?' He did *not* want to go outside and play hockey. Nicky hated getting knocked around. He was always delicate."

It was hard to think of my dad as being delicate. I pictured him strong and good-looking, with long dark brown hair and hazel eyes, smooth skin, and nice white teeth. He wasn't very tall, about five feet nine inches, but he said in his letters that he'd been working out with weights and was in good shape. He always spoke softly, and he really listened to people when they told him something, even me, even when I was a little kid.

"Nicky wasn't a mamma's boy, but he was always thoughtful," Grandma continued. "Same as Hank. He's considerate. I gotta make his lunch when I get home. He's on the midnight shift at the plant."

Grandpa Hank worked at the meat-packing plant on the eastern edge of the city. He commuted twenty miles each way, but he said he liked the trips in and out of town; it gave him time to think and look around. Grandpa Hank was the only man in our family with a job. Grandma and Hank had a little house on a big lot in our old town where they raised and sold chickens and garden stuff.

"Grandma," I asked, "why did Dad get into so much trouble?"

Silence. If it wasn't my birthday and Dad's home-coming, I wouldn't have dared bring up the subject. Grandma always got a hurt look when anyone talked about "Nicky's troubles." Gemma and Mom didn't talk much about it, either, especially to each other.

"Well, Angel, it started when he was your age, actually about eleven or twelve," Grandma said slowly. "I remember that summer like it was yesterday. Your Uncle Al came to stay with us when his momma got so sick. That Al! I do a favour for someone and lose my son over it."

Hardness came into Grandma's usually soft voice. I glanced over at Mom, but she was running her finger around the edge of her glass, as if that was her main focus. Gemma looked pouty. She thought Al and Dad were great, which they were ... sometimes.

"Al was sixteen that summer — and wild. Good-looking and charming! First thing I know, Nick's got

23

money. He's buying candy, chips, and pop for his friends, paying his own way to the movies, buying piles of comic books. Never needed to ask me or Hank for money."

Grandma fanned her face, which had again flamed red from the heat. "I ask where he's getting this money. He says Al and him found work mowing lawns. 'Yeah?' I say. 'For who?' I know everyone in town, but he gives me names I've never heard of. Nicky, he never could lie very good."

"That's why he got into so much trouble and Al didn't," Gemma said.

"That's not why at all!" Grandma snapped. "He wouldn't have *had* to lie if it wasn't for that bad Al putting him up to no good!"

"So where *did* he get the money?" I asked.

"Stealing," Mom said. "He stole anything that wasn't nailed down. Like people's tools or lawn mowers."

"I hope Nick's bus isn't late," Gemma interjected.

"Lawn mowers!" I repeated.

"Yeah, he began his big B and E — breaking and entering — career by breaking into *garden sheds*," Gemma said. "He worked his way up from there to houses, liquor stores —"

"We don't need to go through all this again," Grandma said, her good mood gone. "It gives me heartburn remembering those bad days."

"He said he'd be on the 7:15 bus," Gemma cut in. "He phoned yesterday from the joint. I said I'd meet him."

"He just hero-worshipped that Al," Mom said. "Al was a real bad influence."

"Well, you go ahead and meet him at the bus," Grandma said. "I'll wait here. Someone's got to watch that deep-fat fryer."

"I'll stay with you," Mom volunteered.

I didn't say anything. Mom never went to visit Dad during the whole two years of his incarceration. Only Gemma made regular visits every month.

Grandma sipped on her pink pop. "All his life, Nicky's had bad luck. He thought he was getting somewhere when Al took him into his *business*, but he was blinded by that bad man. Nicky's not bad. He's just unlucky."

"Jerry sees different reasons for Nick's bad luck," Gemma said. "She says the Weasel got slow, and you don't get slow when you're doing a B and E."

"*Shh!*" Grandma hissed. "Don't call him that name! Don't let Angela hear such talk. It's not nice."

"Well, Jerry and I have been seeing each other and he's really a nice guy. So there. Now I'm going to meet my brother at the bus depot! Someone's got to show him we care that he's coming home."

"Nicky will be different when he comes out this time," Grandma said. "He's had lots of time to think in there. And he's got you and Angela to look after. He knows that."

"I'm going to give it everything I've got," Mom said. Her voice sounded so ultra-serious that we all stared at her. "But if any of his ex-con friends start coming around — including Mike and Jerry, I don't care what you say, Gemma — or Uncle Al shows his face, that's it! I don't want Angela to know these people. I don't want her to think what they do is cool. If they come, we're gone."

"Well, isn't that just great!" Gemma's voice slapped across the room. "So Nick's on probation even at home!"

Silence settled, heavier than the heat. I could hardly breathe. It was my fifteenth birthday, and I felt like a hundred and fifteen.

Grandma hoisted herself out of her chair, came around the table, and wrapped her arms around Mom's shoulders. Mom's arms curved partway around Grandma's wide middle, and she rested her head against the pink-flowered dress.

"Oh, Mamma," Mom sighed. "I'm so sorry it's turned out like this. I thought I could help him. I thought he'd straighten up."

"Connie, honey, you're such a good wife for Nicky." Grandma's tone was smooth. "I knew you were special from the minute I met you when you and your folks moved into the big house behind us there. Come on, baby, we'll all help. Me, Hank, Gemma, Angela, all of us. You'll see. Nicky left here a boy. He'll walk in that door a man." Her voice dropped soft and low like a lullaby. "It'll be okay, Connie, honey. It'll be good this time. We'll be a real family again."

I sipped my Coke ... and waited.

3
Birthday

Gemma and I left the house at seven o'clock to get to the bus depot for Dad's 7:15 arrival. I could hardly hold back my excitement. I usually encouraged Gemma to talk about Dad, to tell funny things that she and he did when they were little, but tonight Gemma was tense and didn't feel like talking.

We sat on a bench outside the bus depot, and Gemma pulled out a pack of cigarettes. "Want one?" she asked. I shook my head. She took one out, lit it, using a fancy blue lighter, and shoved the pack inside her purse.

When the bus pulled in, my heart was pounding like crazy. We got up and walked close to the bus door to watch the people get out.

Dad wasn't there.

"Hey!" Gemma called to the driver. "Was there a guy on, dark hair, good-looking?"

"Nope," the driver said.

"You sure?"

"Look, lady, you saw who got off. You don't believe me, go inside and check for yourself."

Gemma did. She came back out with tears in her eyes. "He must have missed the bus. Nick doesn't read clocks too good."

"Maybe Uncle Al drove up to get him," I suggested.

"Nah."

Gemma didn't have to say anything more. It wasn't something Uncle Al would do. He didn't go near jails.

Gemma's mascara was smeared from crying by the time we got home. She really loved her brother and was scared something had happened to him. Me, I just had a hollow ache in my stomach, but it was almost always there.

"He ain't here," Gemma announced as we walked through the door.

Mom and Grandma had the table set, with a bouquet of pink and white peonies in the centre. I could smell their wonderful scent from the doorway, even over the fried chicken.

Quietly, Mom picked up Dad's plate, knife, and fork and put them back in the cupboard.

Grandma, too, was silent — a bad sign.

"Well, happy birthday, baby," Mom said, hugging me.

We celebrated my birthday with fried chicken, potato salad, ice cream, and cake. Grandma gave me money for clothes, and a doll she'd made with a long, fancy skirt. "You gotta put something under her skirt, like a roll of toilet paper, to make her stand up on your dresser," she explained.

Gemma gave me a sample kit of makeup: little tubes of lipstick, eye stuff, and a small bottle of perfume. "I'm starting to get real good at selling this stuff," she said proudly. "I'll make us all beautiful, like me!"

We laughed, but I could see Mom wasn't impressed by Gemma's gift. She thought Gemma wore too much makeup.

Mom's mother and stepfather, Grandma Johnson and her husband Steve, sent me some cool clothes and twenty American dollars. They moved to California to be near my Aunt Jackie after she married a professor who got hired at a university in Santa Barbara. When Mom married Dad, it caused a real split in our family, which was too bad.

By the time Grandma and Gemma were ready to go home, it was almost dark.

"Rain's coming," Grandma announced. "I can smell it."

She was right. An hour later the rain poured down as if it were being dumped from a giant's pail.

Lightning flashed across the black sky followed by the crack of thunder.

"I wonder if Dad's out there trying to hitchhike home," I said to Mom as I got ready for bed.

"I think he knows enough to get out of the rain. You go to sleep, honey. I'll wake you if he shows up."

I lay in bed, listening to the wind and rain that sometimes pounded on the roof, sometimes tapped lightly. I thought of Dad being released today after being in jail for almost two years. When I asked what he was in for, no one would ever tell me the facts.

Mom would say, "A bunch of stupid stuff, never mind."

Gemma would say, "He was part of a famous gold robbery!"

Grandma's response would be: "A bunch of false charges that came from Al's doings. There, now you know."

I still had a lot of questions, the main one being: "Why?"

I could hear Mom pick up her guitar and strum a few chords. I recognized C, F, and G7. Mom was a good musician, and she was teaching me. She'd once recorded a CD, and it was played over several radio stations. But when Mom was in the band, Uncle Al told Dad he'd better watch out, because Mom was so pretty that guys in the audience would be hitting on her all the time.

Dad got scared about that and asked her to quit. I didn't know why she listened to him. Now she just played for me, and sometimes with friends when they came over.

As I fell asleep, I thought about Dad. Maybe he *was* wandering along the side of the highway in the pelting rain and wind and lightning, trying to find his way home. Mom and I could write a sad song about that.

4
Cat

On Monday I walked home from school, wondering what I'd find when I got there. I was waiting for two things: Dad, and my birthday present from Mom. Both were late.

Before I could put my key into the lock the door sprung open. A man stood facing me. I jumped and dropped my keys.

"Oh, Angel, I'm sorry!"

The man scooped up my keys and looked at me. He had short dark brown hair in a buzz cut, hazel eyes, and a moustache. Since he was bare-chested, I could see that his shoulders and chest were muscular. Both of his arms were covered with tattoos. My breathing almost stopped.

"Dad?" I said in a squeaky voice as I put down my backpack.

He held out his arms. I moved ahead stiffly and let him hug me, though it felt weird.

"The door was locked. How'd you get in?"

He grinned. "Wasn't hard." He flipped a small metal object in his hand, shoved it back into the pocket of his jeans, and grinned shyly. "Hey, you're a young lady now. So tall! Beautiful!"

"I'm fifteen."

"Yeah, I know! And I've brought you a present." He searched through a pile of his stuff scattered on the couch and extracted a newspaper-wrapped parcel. "Here!"

I pulled back the paper, and a strange thing peered up at me. It was black with a white face, big staring eyes, and a long black tail. In its belly was a clock.

"Here, I'll show you how it goes." He shoved a battery into the back. The thing began to whir, and the eyeballs flicked back and forth: left, right, left, right, to Dad, to me, to Dad, to me. Its tail was a pendulum switching out the seconds.

"Thought you'd like it," Dad said. "It's Felix the Cat from the cartoons."

"What cartoons?"

"You know — Felix!"

"No."

"Like Garfield, only black. Neat, eh?"

"Yeah, it's cool. Thanks." I held the thing away from me, letting its tail swish, and wondered where I could hang it. Not in my bedroom — too creepy and tacky. "I thought you didn't like clocks."

"Who told you that?"

"Mom."

"Oh." He flashed a smile. "Well, not in jail. You don't think of days or hours in there. You just do your time and get it over with. Now I'm home, so clocks are okay."

After we found a picture nail, hammered it into the living-room wall, and hung Felix, we became shy with each other again. I stared at the jumble of stuff falling out of his duffle bag and wondered what it contained. Old-fashioned clothes that he wore more than two years ago when he was incarcerated? Letters and pictures from me and Gemma? We were the only ones in the family who wrote to him. Did he keep a journal? Did he take courses, or learn to do something that might get him a job when he got out?

"You doing okay in school?" he asked, then looked serious. "Anyone hassling you?"

"No."

"Good. Nobody'd better give you stress. I'll send a posse after 'em."

"Yeah, whatever. You been okay?"

"Me? Oh, yeah. No complaints."

"Anyone hassle you? Give you stress?"

He laughed. "Nope."

"Have you drawn any more pictures?"

He leaped to grab a cardboard-enclosed package. "Here! I brought some home for you."

Out spilled his pictures. The first was done in brown and yellow pastels, a sunset silhouetting a barren tree in the foreground. Nice — until I noted a hangman's noose suspended from one of the dead branches. The second featured black-and-white pastels and had an old Cadillac car with the gangster Al Capone standing in front of it. I knew his face from the million pictures Gemma had collected for Dad and Uncle Al.

"Here's one I did for Valentine's Day," Dad said, "but I didn't know who to send it to."

Dad had used bright poster paints for this one. A man with his fedora hat pulled low over his eyes, cigar held between thumb and forefinger, had a big Valentine heart shaded in behind him. In a "balloon" formed from the cloud of cigar smoke above the man's head, I read: "Just a little Valentine message from Scarface." A gun pointing at the viewer shot a streak of fire.

"That's a Thompson submachine gun," Dad explained. "It's sometimes called a French Broom. The Mob calls it The Typewriter."

"Oh" was all I could say. Like, what was he talking about?

Dad held the picture at arm's length, admiring the three-dimensional effect he'd created. Then he carefully laid it flat on the table. "I'll teach you how to draw, Angel, if you like," he said. "We can start tomorrow. Get you some artist's sketch pads, charcoals, water paints."

"Yeah, I'd like that."

I wouldn't, really. I knew how to paint, but his pictures were disrupting. So was he ... sort of. He didn't seem like the same man who had painted the clowns. But he was my dad, so I loved him. And now he had come home. Maybe for good this time.

5
Canary

Dad and I were sitting at the kitchen table, sipping on cans of Coke, when we heard a car pull up. He jumped up and darted into the living room to peer through the curtain. "Who's that?" he snapped.

"It's Mom!"

"I mean, whose car?"

"I don't know. Maybe someone from work gave her a ride home."

"What's she bringing in?"

A man got out of the car and began hauling a strange contraption from the trunk.

"It's a cage!" I cried. "A birdcage!"

"A what?" Dad asked.

The man handed the cage to Mom, who was carrying a small box and a bag. I ran out to meet her. "Mom,

Dad's home!"

She looked at the man quickly, who nodded good-bye, got into the car, and drove away. "Angela, please don't reveal our home life to others," she said quietly.

"What?"

"That was Jon Percy, my boss. I don't want him knowing anything about me other than that I show up for work on time, and do my job. Understand?"

"Sure. But what's wrong with saying Dad's home ..."

"*Sshh!* Sorry, honey, but that's the way it's got to be. Now — happy birthday!" She held the cage out to me.

"What is it?"

"A *bird*cage. What does it look like?"

"But, we don't have a bird."

"We do now!" She handed me a cardboard box, and I heard a cheeping sound from inside. "Don't open it until we're in the house."

I took the cage and box and raced toward the house. "Mom got me a present!" I yelled to Dad, who'd been spying like a burglar from behind the curtains, but he wasn't looking at me. He was staring straight ahead at Mom as she came up the walk. I went into my bedroom so they could be alone for their first meeting in two years.

Setting the cage on the bed, I opened the little door and then carefully uncovered the box. A bright yellow canary sat inside. He blinked and gazed up at me. "Oh! You're beautiful." Gently, I took him into my hands and stroked his back. He didn't seem afraid. I placed him inside the cage and onto a perch. "I don't care whether you're a boy or girl canary. I'm going to name you Patsy, after Patsy Cline. She's Grandma's favourite singer, and you'll be a singer, too."

Inside the bag were boxes of canary seed and gravel. I filled the little dishes and put them inside. I was just going to the bathroom to fill the water dish when I heard Mom's and Dad's voices. Our house was small, and it wasn't hard to hear every word.

"Sorry I'm late, Con," Dad said. "I stopped to do some shopping."

"Shopping?"

"Yeah, well, I had to see a couple of guys. And I picked up a present for Angela." He must have pointed to the clock. I didn't hear Mom say anything, so I figured she wasn't too impressed.

"Don't you like it?"

"You went *shopping* and *visiting* for three days instead of coming home?"

"Yeah, well, I had to get something for the kid. And I had some business stuff to look after."

Mom still said nothing, but I could tell she was hurt and angry.

"Then I got a ride here with a guy, so it didn't cost me bus fare," Dad continued, "and I brought you a present with the money I saved." I heard a rustle of paper and a gasp from Mom. "Pretty skimpy, huh? I thought you'd look pretty in them."

I imagined Dad had brought her some lacy pajamas.

"Well, are you glad to see me, or not?" Dad's voice was hopeful yet petulant, like a naughty kid wanting instant forgiveness.

Big silence.

Come on, Mom, I thought. *Say it. Say anything, even if you have to lie a little. Make him feel welcome!*

Just when I thought she was never going to speak to him again, I heard her voice, so low I could barely make out the words. "Yes, I'm glad you're home. Everything's fine. Thanks for the ..." Her voice faded, and I realized they might be hugging. *Oh, yeah.*

I turned my attention back to Patsy, who was already pecking at the birdseed. Then I made a noise before I went across to the bathroom to fill the water dish. But Mom and Dad were nowhere in sight.

Lying on my bed, I read *Space-Song* and talked to Patsy. No one seemed to notice that suppertime had come and gone. The only one eating was Patsy, and I didn't feel like sharing birdseed.

Finally, I went into the kitchen and took some cold

chicken from the fridge. I heard voices coming from Mom and Dad's bedroom, so I made lots of noise to remind them that someone else lived in this house besides them. Dad eventually came out of the bedroom. He saw me and smiled.

"Sorry, Angel. Your mom and I were talking over old times. Want me to cook something for supper?"

I smiled. "No, there's a lot left over from my birthday dinner."

When I opened the fridge, he came to stand beside me, looking in awe at its contents. He picked up an egg. "Boy, it's been a long time since I've seen these things. Almost forgot they came in shells." He laughed. "Do you mind if I have a beer? I haven't had one in two years."

"Of course not. Mom bought them for you."

"She did?" Dad seemed pleased. He took one out, flipped open his belt buckle, and expertly used it to snap the cap off the bottle. Fastening his belt again, he spun a kitchen chair around to sit on, then gazed up at me. "Gee, it's good to be home." His eyes darted left to right, as if casing the room, just like those of Felix the Cat. "Home sweet home. I'm never going to leave it again."

Peep! Peep!

Dad tensed. "What's that?"

I ran into my room and brought out the birdcage.

"Who brought that thing in here?" He pointed an

accusing finger at Patsy.

"Dad, what's wrong? It's a yellow canary. Mom bought him for my birthday. I named him Patsy."

"A *canary*! A canary named *Patsy*!" He looked as if he was about to choke.

Mom came out of the bedroom, tying her red silk kimono. "Oh, for Pete's sake, it's only a bird. Drop the jailhouse mentality!"

I didn't understand, but I took my offending present back to my room.

Later Dad came in to explain. "A canary's a sign of a singer, a squealer." He sat on my bed. "That's the lowest form of life. And a patsy's a fall guy, someone set up to take the rap." His voice lowered. "Sometimes, if a patsy tries to get off and sings — tells on the gang — he'll be sent a yellow canary. Usually dead. Like he'll be soon."

I draped a towel over Patsy's cage.

Our home was turning into a halfway house. Mom was trying to guard us from prying outsiders, Dad was home complete with a mental jailhouse attitude, and I was trying to be normal in a house decorated with a spooky wild-eyed clock and pictures of graveyards, hangmen's nooses, and French Brooms.

And now we'd added a yellow canary named Patsy who, the minute his cover was lifted, began to sing his little heart out.

6
Confession

"I'm making breakfast today!" Dad announced. "*Chef de cuisine!*" He began to flip pancakes at high speed. Some drooped crookedly over the edge of the pan, but we pretended not to notice. It was nice having Dad around. Kids needed dads; mothers needed husbands. It made things easier for them, and though my dad wasn't the kind featured on television sitcoms, he was here, he was ours, and he could be fun.

"I'm going to get a job real soon," Dad announced as we sat around the breakfast table. "I'm going to look after this family. You'll see."

"That's nice," Mom said.

"Yeah. I've been thinking ..." Dad began.

"That could be dangerous," Mom said.

"No, honest, I have. I thought about how I got

myself into trouble — all those bad deals — but that's behind me. I'm home for good." He got up to raise the flipper high in the air, tossing three more pancakes that made equally poor landings, then announced, "I'm going to get into business."

"Business!" Mom cried.

"You bet! There are lots of things a guy can do to make money. One fellow I met, he used to install lightning rods on houses. Made a fortune. And another guy designed these little things you use to open any door, or a car, a house, you name it. I bought one, see?" He brought out the little tool he'd used to break into our own house. It looked like a bobby pin.

I shuddered and concentrated on smothering my pancakes with syrup. "So why were all these guys in jail?"

"Oh ... reasons. Some of them weren't too smart. But I studied in there, books and everything. I even learned to type."

"Nick, why don't you take it easy for a couple of days?" Mom suggested. "Something will turn up."

"You could look for a job in the paper," I said.

"I'm not looking for a job in the paper!" Dad's voice was rising. "Those jobs are for idiots. I'm going to do something on my own. You'll see. You'll be real proud of me."

I took my plate and glass to the counter, ran water over them, and gathered my books into my backpack. Then I called out goodbye, but no one seemed to hear.

As I was going out the door, I heard Mom plead, "Start small, Nick, please. Maybe Hank could get you on at the packing plant."

"The packing plant!" Dad yelled. "They *kill* things in there. Innocent animals. You want me to get a job killing animals? No way!"

I closed the door and walked to school. Should I tell Ryan and Hannah that Dad was home? He wasn't going to be an easy person to hide. His tattoos and his manner of dressing and talking were different from other kids' fathers. Hannah's dad wore a tie to mow the lawn!

Hannah was waiting for me in our usual spot in the schoolyard under a big tree outside the main door. She had freckles, pretty, layered blond hair, and brown eyes. Hannah was tall and slim like me, and we looked good together — one blond and one brunette.

"I like your dress," she said. "It's new. Where did you get it?"

"Thanks. My grandma sent it from California. She's my mom's mother."

"I wish I had a grandma who lived there. Do you ever go to stay with her? Check out celebrities' homes?"

"No."

"How come?"

I took a deep breath. "My mom's parents don't like Dad. They don't ever write or phone. They send birthday and Christmas presents to me, that's all."

"Oh."

I waited, my heart pounding. She didn't ask anything more, so I decided to get it over with and tell all. "My dad is ... different, Hannah. He's, well, he's never made very much money. Not like my Aunt Jackie's husband. Uncle Jon teaches at a university in Santa Barbara, and they're rich."

"I thought your dad had a business that took him out of town a lot. A salesman or something. That's an okay job, isn't it?"

"Well, it's not the same as being a professor or a bank manager."

"Oh, well ..."

"My dad just got out of jail."

The words burst out, and I couldn't take them back. I looked away. The sky was clear blue; it was going to be hot again today. Hannah and I sauntered along in step, while I held my breath, waiting for her response to my confession.

"Do you think you can swim with me after school?" she asked. "My mom will drive us out to the lake."

When I dared to look at Hannah through tears that blurred my eyes, she was ambling along as usual, waiting for my answer. Perhaps she hadn't heard what I'd said. But when we turned to go into the school she hugged me, and we continued into our classroom the way best friends should.

7
Reunion

We were eating supper, Mom, Dad, and I, when a quick knock sounded on the door. Dad jumped up, ready for flight.

"Dad! Where are you going?"

His face turned red as he sat down again and Mom went to answer the door.

It was Gemma, Grandma, and Grandpa Hank. When Dad heard their voices, he charged out to greet them. There were big hugs all around. Grandma didn't let go until Dad was squashed and out of breath.

Then it was Gemma's turn. She flung herself into Dad's arms, nearly knocking him off balance. They leaned back to examine each other.

"You're looking great, Nick! You've gained weight. You got a new tattoo! Let's see!" Gemma pulled at

Dad's arm. He jerked back, but Gemma twisted it around to read the message on his left forearm: DEATH BEFORE DISHONOUR.

"Hey, Nick, that's real nice," Gemma said. "Who did it?"

"A guy who used to be in the navy. I met some real artists in there. I thought Uncle Al would like this — a real pro job." Dad reached for Gemma's pack of cigarettes and helped himself to one. "Anyone seen Uncle Al?"

"No!" Grandma's reply was sharp. She sat down with a *whump* on the couch. Hank perched lightly beside her.

Gemma was still examining Dad's tattooed messages. "Here's an entwined *WW*. That stand for Weasel Wroboski?"

"Yeah, I guess so."

"Right on! I'm gonna call you that all the time now. And I want to look at all the pictures you drew. Angela tells me you did a big valentine. Who for — the warden?"

They laughed and joked and punched each other on the arms. I watched everyone else. Mom didn't belong in this room — she was so pretty and classy. Gemma was attractive, but in a category of her own. Grandma loved both of her kids, but she'd heard all their dumb stories and was tired of them. She didn't like how Gemma seemed excited about crime. Hank stayed neutral. He'd said once that he'd married Grandma, not her clan.

While Mom and I cleared away the supper dishes, Gemma and Dad studied his collection of treasures.

"This magazine came out," Dad said, "and I bought every copy in town. Come here, Angel. You should see this. Al Capone's car, a 1930 V-16 Cadillac, one hundred and twenty miles an hour! Bulletproof glass three panes thick. Little portholes in the side windows for shooting through."

Mom stood between me and the bags of stuff. "Angela doesn't need to see this garbage!"

"Aw, Con, I'm just showing the kid some pictures. They're not dirty magazines. They're just cars and guns and dead guys."

Mom sighed heavily.

I went over to sit beside Grandma. She put her arm around me. "Just sit quiet. It'll blow over, honey."

Hank winked at me. He knew how to stay out of the heat.

The evening went okay after that, with everyone being nice. But after Mom served coffee and my leftover birthday cake, Dad got fidgety. He snapped his fingers and nervously tapped his feet on the floor, causing the chains draped around his boot heels to jangle. Then he got up and sat down a couple of times. Finally, he scraped back his chair and stood to do a little boxing dance, punching at the air.

"Hey, Con, if you can lend me some cash, I'll go downtown and get us some beer. Hank, you wanna come?"

Hank appeared stuck for words, so Grandma laid it out for him. "Connie, lend Nick twenty bucks. It'll be good for him to get out of the house. Hank, you go, too. We women will clean up the dishes and talk about you." She chuckled throatily, and tension disappeared like ice on a stove.

When they were gone, the four of us pitched in to clean up. Grandma and I dried dishes — a good time for girl talk.

"Mom, tell us again how you and Dad met," I said.

"Well, first I met Grandma," Mom replied.

Grandma laughed. "Sorry about that!"

"My mother and stepfather, my sister, Jackie, and I, had just moved there," Mom continued. "It was winter. I was walking home from school when I saw this lady —" she indicated Grandma "— outside scooping snow into a bucket. But not just *any* snow. She told me she was looking for *perfect* snow."

"For snow ice cream!" Gemma yelped.

"That's right. And she said I should come in and have some when it was finished."

"Catch a bowl of snow," Grandma said in a singsong voice, "sweeten it with sugar, flavour with vanilla. Add pink or green food colouring, or instant chocolate, or any flavour and colour your heart desires."

"But not *yellow*," Gemma said. "Yellow snow is icky."

"Why?" I asked.

Everyone laughed.

"I want to learn *all* our old family's stories," I said.

"Like how Grandma used to store her chickens over the winter before she had a deep freeze?" Mom asked. "I nearly fainted when I stumbled on her *cache*."

"Where?"

"You know Grandma has always raised chickens," Mom continued. "She'd wait until the snow was deep and the temperature real low in early winter before she slaughtered them. Then she'd chop off their heads over an old log and stick the bodies into the snowbank."

"The yard was fenced real good to keep out dogs or coyotes," Gemma added.

"So she'd bury the chickens in the snow and then dig one out when she wanted to cook it for supper," Mom said. "I went over once when the temperature suddenly turned warm. There was Grandma up to her knees in slush, looking for her buried chickens. She'd find one, pull it out, and throw it into the washtub — feathers, feet, and all. Then she covered them with ice she bought from the gas station."

"Gross," I said.

"That was what it was like in those days," Grandma said. "We didn't have running water and electric lights till long after the city got them. And we didn't have money, either. Couldn't go to the store and just buy everything."

"Mamma could make us a meal out of wild greens and berries if she had to," Gemma said. "I still get a craving for them."

"My mamma and poppa came from the old country," Grandma said. "They were poor and couldn't afford doctors. She taught me lots of things about homemade cures that she'd learned from her mamma."

Gemma giggled. "Remember when Connie came berry-picking with us? She was so prim and proper — until she cut her foot. Blood everywhere. Mamma yells, 'Connie, whip off your halter top!' Connie, she didn't know what for, she's all embarrassed, but she does it. Mamma ties it like a tourniquet around her foot. Then Mamma sends me to find a puffball, and we sprinkle the dust on Connie's foot."

"The bleeding stopped just like that," Mom said. "I could hardly believe it."

"Better not get puffball dust in your eyes, though," Grandma warned. "It's no good at all for eyes. Now where do you think those men have got to? It's getting late. Hank has to work at midnight, and I have to make his lunch yet."

"It's only nine o'clock," Gemma said. "Almost party time."

"Maybe for you," Grandma said. "Not for me. And not for Angela. The young and the old need their beauty sleep, right, Angel?"

I nodded, but I didn't want to go to bed yet, either. It was hot and still mostly daylight. And I had a feeling that when Dad and Hank came back, they wouldn't be alone.

8
Party

I was just getting ready for bed when Dad came roaring back.

"Grab your guitar, Con!" he yelled to Mom. "It's party time!"

Something, likely a case of beer, was plunked onto the table, and I heard people coming up the walk. The voices of two of Mom's old musician friends, Calvin Major and Conor Gill, were familiar. They'd likely brought their banjo, harmonicas, and guitars.

When I heard Mom tune up her guitar, I threw on my clothes again and snuck into the living room as she and the musicians broke into a bluegrass tune. Mom had a great voice, and the musicians were really lively. Dad saw me standing against the wall, came over, snatched my hand, and whirled me into the room.

"Nick, take it easy!" Grandma cried, but she was laughing.

Dad was a good dancer, and so was I. In the country and small towns people took their kids to lots of socials. Grandma and Hank got up and took a turn, too. I danced with Dad, then with Hank. After that Gemma grabbed me, and we twirled around the room.

"Can you take over the music, Angel?" Dad asked. "I want to dance with your mom."

I picked up Mom's big Gibson flat-top guitar and started to play. Calvin called over, "Key of G," and away we went.

Everyone was having a great time. Dad did some fancy steps, and Mom shook her skirt like a flamenco dancer. I laughed and sang along with Conor and Calvin.

Finally, Mom was breathless from dancing and took the guitar from my hands. "That's enough for tonight. It's nearly eleven o'clock. Angela's way overdue for bedtime, and the rest of us have to get up early. Hank has to be at work in an hour. Last song!"

Mom and I sang "Grandpa" in harmony, made popular by The Judds. We looked right at Grandpa Hank, and he got teary-eyed. Then the musicians packed up their instruments, and everyone said good-night.

I went to bed feeling great. We *could* have a lot of fun together. As I drifted off to sleep, I heard Mom and

Dad talking as they cleaned up the living room.

"Great party, eh, babe?" Dad said. "All that music and dancing." He paused, and I was nearly asleep when his next comment brought me wide awake again. "I wonder where Uncle Al is? I haven't heard from him. He around?"

That familiar ache started in my stomach, sharp, hollow, filling my body with dread.

Mom's voice was tense as she said, "I wouldn't know. I haven't seen him and I don't want you to see him."

"Aw, Connie, I wish you'd change your mind about Uncle Al. He's —"

"A jerk!"

"An okay guy. He can come up with bail money faster than anyone."

I heard Mom slap something down on the table. "It took me a year to pay him back for your lawyer, plus interest!"

"Uncle Al's a businessman."

"I'll say. It was his rap you took. I'll never forgive him — or you for being so dumb."

"It got complicated, that's all. But it's over."

There was silence for a moment, then Dad said, softer now, "You know, Connie, lying on my bunk in that cell all those months, I used to wonder what you ever saw in me, why you picked me."

Silence.

"Why did you?"

"Who knows?" Mom sounded tired. "I think Grandma pulled a 'snow job' on me, talking about how good-hearted you were, how misunderstood. And then I met you — and you seemed to walk different."

"I what?"

"You walked different. You see a litter of puppies; you don't know which one to pick. Then one trots over and something about him makes him stand out from the rest. And you've got to have that one."

"Maybe a little cuter than the others, eh?"

"Or a little crazier. Or more pathetic. I guess I was rebelling, too, from my parents, and you seemed to be on my side."

"Everyone needs someone. Needs a break. Now if I could just get one good break-in."

"You mean *break*. You said *break-in*."

"What? Yeah. Break. I meant break."

Mom's voice became hard again. "Do me a favour, Nick. For me and for Angela. Just *don't*, okay?"

"Sure, it'll keep. You ready to go to bed?"

I heard Dad go into the bedroom. Mom shut off the lights and went to the bathroom. The ache receded a bit and I fell asleep.

9
Betrayal

Patsy's singing woke me. I'd slept in! It was 9:30! Sunlight streamed through my window. There were no sounds in the house. Why hadn't someone wakened me? I was late for school!

I had just touched my feet on the floor when I heard a sharp knock on the front door. Was I the only one home? I pulled on my housecoat, planning to answer it when I heard footsteps cross the living-room floor. Opening my bedroom door a crack, I saw Dad peering through the curtains, checking to see who was there. He gave a shout and flung open the door.

A huge man stood on the step. He was wearing a black trench coat, a shirt open at the collar, dark dress pants, and patent leather shoes and was carrying a brief-case. He looked rich ... and scary.

Uncle Al had come to call.

Dad and Uncle Al hugged, held back, sized each other up, and punched shoulders.

What could I do?

I didn't have time to decide. Uncle Al spotted me peeking out my door. "Angela!" he called. "Hey, Nick, what's the little gal doing home? Doesn't she go to school anymore?"

"Oh, no!" Dad whirled around. "Sorry, Angel. I got up with Connie. She told me to let you sleep another half-hour. Guess I forgot to look at the clock."

"We're having a math test today!" I yelped. "It's our year-end final. I'll fail if I miss it."

"Quick! I'll make your lunch. You get ready."

I brushed my teeth and hair, washed my face, and pulled on a skirt, tank top, and sandals. I grabbed an apple and the baloney sandwich Dad had thrown together and was out the door in ten minutes, wondering if Mom would be told about this visit from Uncle Al. Should I tell her if Dad didn't?

Before going into the classroom I had to get a late slip from the secretary. They'd already begun the test, so Mrs. Madsen motioned me to wait by the door. In a moment she came out, looking cross. "Where have you *been*, Angela? How come you're late?"

I handed her the note. On it was my excuse — slept in.

She frowned. "This is really too bad. There's not enough time for you to score more than forty percent at the most."

"Please, can I write it, anyway? I've studied."

"All right, but I'll have to send a note home to your mother about this. It could mean a low grade in math, which will pull down your grade-point average. And you were up for the Honour Roll, you know ..."

I nodded, took the test paper, and sat at my desk. Hannah raised her eyes and quickly lowered them again. I glanced across the room at Ryan. He gave me a quick smile. I managed a weak one in return and started the test.

When the bell rang, we all handed in our papers. Mine was half-finished. It wouldn't be enough to pass because I probably hadn't gotten everything right.

Hannah waited for me at the door. "How come you were late, Angela? I waited for you under the tree until I was nearly late myself."

"Dad was supposed to wake me, but he forgot."

Ryan was talking to someone else, so Hannah and I walked outside and stood at the edge of the school grounds.

Hannah studied her shoes. "Angela, there's something I have to tell you. Dad asked me last night about your father. I guess he came into Dad's bank yesterday with a cheque that wasn't good."

I felt my face flame. "How could he? He just got home."

She sighed. "Maybe he went there on his way home. Anyway, the cheque your dad tried to pass was on an account that had been cancelled two years ago! Really, Angela. We're friends and everything, but I don't know why your dad would try to rip us off."

I could hardly breathe. "It must have been a mistake."

"Well, maybe. But when Dad asked me about him I had to tell him, you know, what you told me yesterday."

"You *what*? That was a secret! I trusted you!"

"He's my *father*, Angela. And it's his bank. He's the manager. He's responsible. I can't lie to him, not even for a friend. It's not right." She stopped to let that sink in.

I gazed out over the schoolyard. Kids were running around having a good time, sitting on picnic tables, planning their summer vacations, gossiping about boys — all the things I wasn't doing. Some were throwing a basketball through an outdoor hoop; others were kicking a soccer ball around the field. I wanted to join them. I wanted to run and yell and kick the ball so hard that it exploded. My stomach was on fire, and my throat felt as if I'd swallowed my heart. I blinked fast. No way would she or anyone see me cry over embarrassment about my dad.

When I could finally speak, I said, "So what did your father say about what happened at the bank?" I continued to watch the kids playing ball. My eyes flitted back and forth like my Felix clock.

"Well ..." Hannah scuffed dust with the toe of her shoe, making little trails in the ground.

"You can't hang around with me, right?"

"Not exactly. He just said I wasn't to go to your house anymore, that's all. You can still come to mine."

"So I guess the idea of you coming to my house for a sleepover is out."

Hannah looked away.

I thought about going into their fancy house, saying hello to her parents and to her older brothers, everyone knowing that my dad was an ex-con who had tried to pass a bad cheque.

"We could meet at the pool or at movie theatres," she suggested.

I could sense that now *she* was trying hard not to cry. I was past that. The lump in my throat had gone into my stomach where it sat hard and hot. *Jailbird's kid.* So that was what it meant. I blinked back another wave of shame.

Then I thought of last night, dancing with Dad while Mom played her guitar and sang. I thought of Grandma telling stories about the old days, of Grandpa Hank sitting beside her, happy to watch and listen, tapping his toes to the music. Calvin and Conor and I playing songs on harmonicas and banjos and guitars. Gemma whooping and hollering around the room, her strong perfume and cigarette smoke making the room smell all close and homey.

Tears now spilled from my eyes. I turned to Hannah. "I love my family!" I said, choking out the words. "My dad isn't a bad person. This is the first time I've seen him in two years. We don't know each other that well, but I'm going to give him a chance."

I stopped talking and took a deep, shuddering breath. Hannah was silent. I glanced over, but her eyes were fixed on other people in the schoolyard. I, too, watched the soccer game, which was getting rougher. The ball made loud thunks as it was being kicked.

"Hannah, I'm going inside to talk to Mrs. Madsen about the math test. See you."

I turned and walked into the school, not looking back.

10
Class

The front door to our house was wide open when I returned from school. Flies buzzed in and out. Country music blared from the radio. Gemma and Dad were sitting at the kitchen table, drinking beer, talking, and smoking.

"Hey, kid, how are ya?" Gemma yelled when she saw me. "Your old man and me are having a good day. I beat him three straight games at crib."

I smiled and went into my bedroom. It was hot even with all the windows open. Patsy sat still on his perch, greeting me with a couple of drowsy cheeps.

Tomorrow I had a geography exam and had to study for it. All year I'd had good marks, but I was worried about the finals, especially after the math test today. I wanted to be on the honours list. Hannah and I always did our homework projects together. I wished I could go over to her house to study, but I couldn't, and it was hard to concentrate here with the noise and heat.

I called Ryan, but no one answered, and I didn't leave a message. Lying back on my bed, I opened a book. I'd been reading the same page over and over when I became aware that the only sound in the house was coming from the radio. I got up to investigate.

Dad and Gemma were sitting at the table with their heads bent together: Gemma's hair was no longer bleached blond but dyed brown with tinges of red; Dad's was rich dark brown and buzzed short, the kind of criminal cut I'd seen in movies.

"What are you doing?" My voice startled them, and they looked up.

On a sheet of waxed paper were a bottle of black calligraphy ink, some sewing needles, and a spool of white thread.

"Your dad's giving me a tattoo!" Gemma shouted over the music. "He's good! I want one before he gets famous and charges for it!"

They both laughed. Dad focused on winding thread around two needles. Curious, I sat down to watch.

"Just where my little finger starts, Nick," Gemma said. "That's where the bird's wings should go, so I can make them flap."

"Hold still." Dad bent his head, concentrating on his work. He dipped the bound needles into the ink and then punctured them into her hand, following a picture he'd outlined in pen. Over and over. Gemma didn't seem to feel the pain, but I did.

"One wing reaching up to this knuckle, the other up the next. There. It'll fly!" He held her hand up toward the light to check his work.

"You gonna write something under it?" Gemma asked.

"Naw. Looks classier, just the picture. You don't want writing."

"Mamma's gonna have a fit," Gemma said. "She said no more tattoos. One's all right, but more than one looks cheap. You remember that, Angela."

"Yeah, sure."

"Aw, don't worry about Mamma," Dad said. "You are what you are."

"Connie's teaching me and Angela to be classy," Gemma said, with a wink at me.

Dad glanced up. "Yeah? How?"

"Well, once when I was going through the Avon catalogue, I was buying this lipstick for myself, and Connie says, 'No, Gemma, pay a dollar more and get the gold tube with the flowers on it.' I was gonna buy the one in the pink plastic tube, see. Same lipstick, dollar cheaper."

"Makes sense."

"But Connie says, 'You buy the expensive one, and every time you take it out — in the can at the hotel, or in a café or at work — people will notice it and say it's nice.' Isn't that right, Angela?"

"Sure. Mom says we might be broke, but we don't have to look poor."

"Now I advise my customers at the store to buy the more expensive things. My manager likes that."

"Yeah, Con, she's always been like that," Dad said. "She buys good stuff. She likes fancy dishes and things, too."

"And she told me, 'Gemma, buy *lace* underwear.'"

Dad laughed and opened another bottle of ink — red this time. He sterilized the needles in a pot of boiled water, rewound new thread around them, and dipped the needles into the red ink. "This is an oriole. Need a touch of red for the wings. They're nice birds."

"How come Uncle Al hasn't come around?" Gemma asked suddenly.

Dad didn't look up. "I don't know. I haven't seen him. Connie doesn't like him much. She said I got this choice — me or him. So I had to tell Uncle Al to find a new partner —"

"I thought you said you ain't seen him," Gemma said.

Dad was trapped. It was time to make a snack, so I opened the fridge door. Mom's groceries had been pushed aside to make room for a case of beer and a pizza with two slices missing. I took a piece of pizza and ate it cold. *Yum!*

"You gonna find a job?" Gemma asked. Then she cried, "Ouch!" as Dad's needles hit a sensitive spot on her outstretched hand.

"Hold still," Dad said. "Yeah, I'm planning to."

"What kind of job do you want to get this time, Dad?" I asked.

"Oh, I'd like to get back working at the graveyard for starters."

"You were good at it," Gemma said. "You were kind to those people."

"Who can you be kind to at a graveyard?" I asked. "Everyone's dead."

"Don't matter," Dad said. "I was nice to them, anyway. If my shovel loosened a chunk of dirt when I was digging the next grave over, sometimes their neighbour would fall into the new hole. So I'd tuck his old bones back where they belonged. Keep things neat."

"Oh, that's real nice," Gemma said.

"Yeah, I'll go down to the city yard office tomorrow after Connie gets my pants pressed. I've got to look good, even if it's just to apply for a grave-digging job. Like Con says, you have to show class."

"Mom doesn't like you to call her Con," I said. "She doesn't like that word."

Gemma and Dad stared at me.

I stared back. Dad sat bare-chested, tattoos trailing down both arms. And I saw other scars, too. There were criss-cross cuts on his forearms and even some across his chest.

"Aw, Connie gets funny ideas," Gemma said. "I wished she'd be nicer to Jerry. He's a good guy."

"No, he's not," Dad said. "Get rid of him."

"Hey, you got no right to say that. Jerry and Mike and you did a lot of jobs together."

"*Shh!*" Dad said, flicking his eyes toward me. "No more of that stuff. That's past. Angela and Connie are depending on me."

"Yeah, right," Gemma said in a tone I didn't like.

By the time Mom came home, Gemma had left, the table was set for supper, the pizza was warming in the oven, and I'd made a salad.

"Wow!" Mom said. "This is great."

"Here, Con — uh, Connie — let me take your purse, those groceries," Dad said, jumping up. "You hop into the shower, change into something cool. We'll eat outside, like a picnic. Here, take a beer into the shower with you."

Mom laughed, and Dad laughed back. *Cool.*

11
Comics

Ryan and I planned to get together at his house every day from now until exams were over. He was smart and liked to study lots.

I finally got up the nerve to tell him about Dad. He blinked as he thought over what I'd told him. "Whoa, really?" he finally said.

"Yeah, really." I'd already lost communication with one friend because of Dad. If I lost Ryan, I'd be alone.

"That's kind of neat," he said.

I relaxed.

"Let's take a break from this." Ryan logged onto his computer, using a password to gain access to some interesting sites. When the computer asked for "Destination," I saw one called "Escape."

I laughed. "Hey, Dad would be interested in that option!"

"It's not exactly related to prison escapes," he said with a smile.

It was great to be able to joke instead of freaking out about the subject.

Ryan was a total fan of comics, so we checked out some new posts on a nerdy web forum that Ryan was involved in to get the weekly updates on his favourite characters.

"Comics are really changing," Ryan informed me. "Even Superman — new look, new powers. He doesn't fly anymore. He *transports*. Bullets go through him instead of bouncing off. Totally electronic. It's all right, I guess, but some fans don't like it."

"Look, Super Pets!" I read lists of new monsters that would be appearing in upcoming comic books.

"Yeah, people of all ages are enjoying comics now." He grinned. "Even bank managers. It's all about having super powers, large muscles ..."

A fantastic thought jumped into my head. "Dad would love it."

Ryan glanced at me. "Yeah? Your dad into this stuff?"

"He would be if he saw this. Look at these illustrations. Dad loves to create and draw characters — villains, heroes, weird creatures!"

"Let's print some of this for you to take home," Ryan offered.

"Go for it!" I ordered.

"We've got to get a computer," I said, "but they cost a lot of money. Maybe someday when things are different."

"You can come and use mine anytime," Ryan said. "No cost. Mom won't care. I spend a couple of hours a day surfing the Net, anyway. Tell your dad to come over here sometime. You said he likes to draw pictures. What of?"

"Weird stuff." I tried to describe Dad's art.

"Anything like this?" he asked, and DragonLance Pictures flashed onto the screen. "I've read about fifty of these books. I know all the writers and the artists. Look."

We scanned through book titles and descriptions and drawings of huge green, silver, and white dragons with piercing eyes and flaming nostrils. Heroes wielded swords and lances to slash at minotaurs. Dark queens came to life surrounded by mischievous dwarves, generals, and knights. And there were evil barbarians and beautiful, victimized heroines.

"Yes!" I shouted as the printed images rolled out. "This could be Dad's future! These are the kinds of things he was born to do." If help came through images of dragons, heroes, and villains, then I'd praise the cyber-world forever.

Ryan laughed. "Well, if he wants to borrow my comic books or ask me about this stuff, I'll bring over a box full." He turned in his swivel chair to face me. "I'll help all I can, Angela. You're the first close friend I've ever had. I don't have a dad. I mean, I do, but I've never seen him. He left Mom when I was a year old." There was a catch in his voice. "Maybe your dad isn't perfect, but he's there now. And I'm sure he cares a lot about you."

I stared hard at the computer screen. Laurana, flying over a high mountain peak astride the fire-breathing Silver Dragon, wavered and then faded.

Ryan busied himself clicking the mouse. "Let's see if I can find anything about prisons."

I followed his search. We found book titles with intriguing names: *Waiting for the Ice Cream Man, Shaking It Rough, Prisoners of Isolation*. I made a note to look them up in the library to learn more about what Dad had been through.

"Is there anything on the Net about helping ex-cons find jobs?" I asked.

We put out a query on a chat line and were told about the John Howard Society, Seven Steps programs, and others.

"Is your dad on parole?" Ryan asked.

"No, he served his full sentence. He's free."

"Oh, then it looks like he's on his own. These groups will help if someone's on parole or are going to be getting out of prison and need halfway houses or something."

I sighed. "Yeah, he's on his own, and that's why he needs *us*."

We also discovered there were papers written and talks given on subjects such as "Women on the Outside" for wives, girlfriends, or mothers of inmates. "What about 'Kids on the Outside'? I asked, but could find nothing.

"Maybe you should write something," Ryan suggested.

"Maybe I will."

Two hours passed, and we had hardly opened our textbooks to study for tomorrow's test. In the next half-hour we crammed in a day's worth of studying.

I walked home, carrying a stack of information. I'd gained a lot more than a study partner. Ryan was a true friend. He'd offered help when I really needed it.

12
Business

The second last week of June we went to school only to write exams, so I had most afternoons free. When I got home, I found the door locked. Dad must have gone out looking for a job!

I let myself in and went into my bedroom. There were voices outside in the backyard. I peered out my window and saw Dad and Uncle Al sitting at the picnic table, drinking coffee. They were talking in low voices. I watched them without being observed by peeking through my sheer curtain and heard them quite plainly through the open window.

I wish I hadn't.

"Well, I meant to come around, see how Con was getting on while you were in the slammer," Uncle Al was saying to Dad, "but then I got busy. And I know

Con doesn't like me much."

"She doesn't know you," Dad said.

Uncle Al laughed. "Yeah, right. Well, Con's entitled to her opinions. She's done okay with her job and everything. And I've got my own business to run."

"You look like a millionaire."

He and Uncle Al sure didn't seem related. Dad was bare-chested and barefoot and wore only a pair of knee-slashed jeans. Uncle Al's light blue golf shirt had a little collar and a crocodile emblem on the front, and he wore white pants with a perfect crease. His black hair was neatly cut and styled.

Uncle Al's laugh was deep and diabolical. "Well, I've got a good deal going. And it's even legal, Your Honour! Business licence and everything. Called Dial-a-Dream."

"What do you do?"

"Personal deliveries — booze, mix, party stuff. When I started out, I called it Dial-a-Party, but cops hassled me all the time. I told them to leave honest citizens alone and go after the crooks."

Uncle Al sounded hurt and indignant. Dad shook his head in agreement with Al's reason for annoyance.

"Now, *you*." Uncle Al leaned forward, his tone suddenly business-like. "We've got to set you up in something. If you can get some dough together, maybe you can even buy into the business."

"I might have a job," Dad said. "Angela printed me some information off the computer about night courses I could take. She thinks I could learn how to draw on computers and sell the pictures for book covers and illustrate comic books."

"Hey, that's a *hobby*," Uncle Al said. "I'm talking *business* here. Wouldn't you like to own a business and do your drawings on a computer? We can get everything you need, drawing programs, you name it. Hot computers are a dime a dozen — I could get you anything you want. You can learn and work at the same time."

"Yeah?" Dad sounded pathetically hopeful.

"Yeah." Uncle Al took a sip of coffee. "Excuse me." He slowly stood, stretched, and came into the house, likely to use the bathroom.

I sat back, wishing I'd thought to close my bedroom door. I couldn't get up and do it now. He would see me.

"Hello there, Angela." Uncle Al was standing in the doorway. "Get home early from school?" There was a little smile on his face.

"Yeah, we're just writing exams this week."

"How are you doing?"

"All right."

Uncle Al took out a money clip, flipped through some twenty- and fifty-dollar bills, and threw a fifty onto my bed. "Here. Early graduation present. Buy yourself something nice." He winked and went into the bathroom.

I quietly closed my bedroom door. In a couple of minutes I heard him go out.

"I've gotta split," he said to Dad. "Got a business to look after."

I had to keep everything straight in my mind. I hadn't told Mom that Uncle Al was here the other day. And I couldn't let Dad know I'd overheard him and Uncle Al discussing *business*. I'd heard the expression *hush money*. Now I knew what it meant. I had fifty dollars' worth in my pocket.

13
Heroes

We finished writing exams at school. Soon it would be our final sports day and picnic. I was entered in almost all track events because I was good and fast and wanted to win.

As I hurried out of the room after the last exam was finished, Hannah caught up to me and tugged my arm to make me stop. Her usually happy brown eyes were big and sad. "Angela, we've got to talk."

"I can't. I have to practise."

"I'll walk you to the jumping pit."

We strode along together, but for once we didn't have anything to say. While I waited for the teacher to rake the sand pit so he could measure our distances in the long jump, Hannah suddenly said, "Angela, I'm really sorry."

"About what?"

"About your dad. I shouldn't have told."

"It's okay. I'm not going to hide things anymore. I shouldn't have said he was an out-of-town businessman."

"If you hadn't, maybe we wouldn't have gotten to know each other ..." She hesitated, trying not to say what we were both thinking. If she'd known Dad was in jail when I moved here, she wouldn't have made friends with me in the first place.

"Don't worry about it," I said, pretending not to care, then lined up to make a jump.

She watched for a while and finally left. I didn't look after her until I knew she was too far away to notice. Hannah was trailing a stick in the dirt, like a leash with no dog, trudging slowly through the school grounds. She looked lonelier than I did.

I had lots of company now. The track team had been practising every afternoon, I often went over to Ryan's, and now with Dad being home, I was never alone.

Dad didn't seem to be making much effort to look for a job. He mostly hung around the house, drinking coffee in the morning and switching to beer in the late afternoon as he shuffled through his magazines and artwork stored in an old trunk. He called it "taking inventory."

When I got home from track practice, Dad tried to get me to check out his material. So I did to please him. "What are the markers for in these magazines?" I asked.

"Those are stories about my favourite people — Al Capone, Dutch Schultz, Lucky Luciano, you know, the big guys."

"Oh."

"And this mag features Al Capone's tunnels. They ran from the Lexington Hotel in Chicago to all the speakeasies and bookie joints. This map shows secret exits from his gaming rooms."

"I don't know what you're talking about."

"Well, take a look here." He spread open the magazine to display pictures of fierce men with hats pulled low and guns pointed. There were scenes of massacres, of dead bodies hanging out of car doors or lying on streets in pools of blood.

"What do you *see* in these things?" I asked. "Who *are* these men?"

"Heroes," Dad said.

I hesitated to do it, but I asked Ryan if he could pull any material about the Mob from the Internet.

He looked away, his face reddening. "Sure, Angela."

I swore to myself that I'd never again ask him to get me stuff like this. From now on I'd concentrate on real heroes, people my dad should admire and learn from — like Dr. Phil or Oprah.

Later Ryan handed me an envelope containing print-outs on movies, books, and television shows featuring various Mafia members and their crimes. I thanked him and quickly stuffed the envelope into my backpack.

I knew that re-educating Dad was going to involve a major learning process, especially when I returned home to see him sorting pictures and stories about one of his favourites — Machine Gun Kelly.

"You won't believe this, Angela," he said, flipping a well-worn page, "but Machine Gun Kelly never actually killed anybody. He's just like me."

"Huh?"

"I'd never kill anyone, either. I couldn't even help Mamma butcher her chickens. And Con thinks I should ask Hank to find me a job in the packing plant! Never! Never! No way." Dad closed the magazine, slid it back into its protective plastic envelope, and took out his drawings. "These are ones I did while I was in the jug." He was referring to his last stay at Fort Gavin prison. "This here's Smiley. He was a guard. A good fella, Smiley." Dad handed over his portrait of a nice-looking gentleman.

"Most inmates don't like guards, but Smiley's different. All the guys talked to him. When I did his picture and he showed it around, the guys asked me if I'd draw *their* pictures. Then they sent 'em to their girls or their wives — or both." Dad laughed.

He put down other sketches he'd made — of men with no smiles, men with no teeth, men with hair cut short like Dad's or hanging long and scraggly, some in braids, some in ponytails. Men with big ears, crooked noses, bushy eyebrows, squinting eyes, tattooed chests, backs, and arms.

We were so busy looking at Dad's artwork that we didn't hear someone come up the steps. Suddenly, Uncle Al burst into the room. I jumped, and Dad let out a holler.

"Hey, you're getting slow, Weasel. Just like Mike said. I could have knocked over the joint and you wouldn't have even looked up." Uncle Al slapped Dad on the shoulder and winked at me. "Hi, Angela. Hey, what have you got there?" He picked up a picture and then a second one. "Weasel, these yours? They're *good*!"

"Yeah? You think so?" Dad glanced up, a pleased look on his face.

Uncle Al picked up another, and another. "You could do this for a living."

"That's what the warden said. He had me paint a mural on the wall in the cafeteria. But naw, I don't think there's any money in this."

"Well, yeah! There's got to be a buck in it somewhere. Like I said, you got talent. How did you do these pictures of all these guys? They pose for you?"

"No, no. They'd ask me to do their picture. I'd take a good look at a guy, then go back to my room, do some sketches. They'd give me something for them — smokes and stuff. I can remember details real good. I drew this one of the warden's office. I was just there once, but look." He pulled a picture from the bottom of the stack. It was of an office, complete to the last detail. "You see this fancy thing on his desk? It's made of silver, an ornament. You push it, and this whirligig goes around."

"And you remembered it, perfectly," Uncle Al said, "and then you drew it."

"Yeah, everything. And the warden, too. That's exactly what he looks like. What's the big deal?"

Uncle Al did a little dance around the table, holding the picture in front of him. He brought it to his lips, kissed it, and held it up toward the window.

"What are you *doing*, Al?" Dad stood and tried to retrieve the picture.

Uncle Al stopped in front of me. "Do you know what your dad is, Angela? He's a *professional artist*!" He turned to Dad. "You can case joints, Weasel, study and draw plans of these places, just like an architect. You can be a 'weasel,' a front-runner."

"Al, not in front of Angela!"

Uncle Al glanced at me. "Don't worry about Angela. She's okay. She doesn't understand — and further, she's *family*! Weasel, you can —"

"And don't call me that in front of Angela."

"Think smart, Nick. Think dollars. Think of your *family*."

He released his hold on Dad's picture, pulled out a chair, and sat down. I'd been somehow included in this plot, and there was no way I could leave. I looked at Dad's pictures, examining the faces of the men.

"You look a place over and then you come home and *draw* it," Uncle Al said. "You get the windows, where the furniture is, entrances, exits. We study your drawings, put them on a computer even, and then figure out what we need. Guns, ammunition, ropes, saws, dynamite —"

"Dynamite!" I exclaimed.

"Angela, get out of here!" Dad said.

"An axe, screwdrivers," Uncle Al continued.

The expressions on their faces made me feel sick. My stomach knotted as Dad's eyes lit up with excitement and Uncle Al's face turned sly, his attention totally focused as if he were a surgeon over an operating table.

"Dad!" I shouted.

"Angela," Dad said quietly, "this is business."

"You can make maps," Uncle Al went on as if neither of us had spoken. "You and me, we're a *team*, Nick. We think things through, talk them out, draw them, every little detail. Put them on a computer, look for trouble spots. You think Al Capone just blasted into a place? No! He planned, organized, got stuff down on paper ..."

87

"Not his taxes," Dad said.

"He didn't leave nothing to chance. You and me, Weasel — sorry, *Nick* — from here on, we're going to go professional." He sat back, propped his big hands on his knees, his lion head thrown back, and flicked his sharp black eyes from Dad to me, waiting for Dad's response, daring me to interrupt men's business.

"Sure, Al," I heard Dad say. "So, uh, what are we doing, *professional?*"

Uncle Al looked around as if checking doors and windows. Then he leaned forward and whispered, "We're going to *do* the bank machines."

I couldn't breathe. If I opened my mouth, I'd be sick.

"What?" Dad's features were smooth, his eyes innocent like those of a man with a hearing problem. But I'd heard. I didn't know what *do* meant, but I knew what bank machines were. They were usually in a room by themselves just inside the main door of the bank. You pushed some buttons and out came your money.

"Get me some paper and a pen!" Uncle Al ordered.

Zombie-like, I rose, got a pencil and a sheet of paper from my backpack, and handed them to Uncle Al.

"Okay, here's the layout," Uncle Al said. "The first bank you should case is on Seventh Street, see. That runs north and south."

I stood and went into my room. I didn't slam the door, though. I was scared of Uncle Al, and maybe Dad was, too. What made a person so powerful that others rushed to obey his orders no matter how crazy they were? I had to think about this.

When I took Patsy's cage off the chain in front of the window and set it on my bed, he hopped toward me on his perch.

I wanted to tell Mom that Uncle Al had been here. That he had given me money. That he was trying to get Dad to do another stupid bank job. But if I did, Mom would get totally angry, she and Dad would fight, and he'd get kicked out. Then Uncle Al would really own him.

Grandma would know what to do. I had to talk to her. Grandma had known Uncle Al longer than any of us. I decided to ask if I could go out there on Saturday.

I returned to the kitchen to start supper. Uncle Al and Dad were still sitting around the table, with Dad's artwork spread out.

"Why are we robbing the bank machines instead of the tellers like always?" Dad suddenly asked.

Big question.

"Because it's *easier*, Weasel." Uncle Al's voice was soft and coaxing, as if he were trying to get a baby to eat spinach. "It's the new way. Nobody smart robs tellers anymore. They've got too many alarms, even silent ones that only ring in a police station. Spy cameras. Dirty tricks like that."

"That's cheating!"

"Yeah, right you are, Weasel."

They both nodded sympathetically. I couldn't believe my dad could act so dumb.

"Also, the banks are *insured* against robbery," Uncle Al continued in a smooth voice. "They *expect* to be robbed. They get the money back from the insurance company, so the poor schmucks who stick in their fifty bucks a week don't lose their savings."

I didn't want to hear any more of their stupid talk. I banged pots around until Dad suddenly said, "Holy smoke, Con will be home soon!"

Uncle Al stood, gathered his cigarettes and his silver lighter, and grabbed his sports jacket where he'd flung it over a chair. "You're a real little helper, Angela," he said, coming over to the counter. "A smart kid. Your momma and daddy are lucky to have a good girl like you. And I know you want them to be happy."

I didn't say anything.

"You know what'll make them *really* happy is your daddy getting a job. Right?"

"He *will* get a job!" I said. "He's planning to learn computers — and he's going out tomorrow to apply for a real job. He wants to dig graves for the city again. He liked that. He was good at it."

Uncle Al's laughter exploded. "That's a good one! Hey, Weasel, you're not serious about grave-digging, are you? No one's buried anymore with jewellery on 'em. No one even has gold teeth worth claiming!"

Dad laughed, and I wish he hadn't. It wasn't funny at all.

Uncle Al went out the door, still laughing, and jumped into a big black car with DIAL-A-DREAM written on the sides in bright pink letters. He gunned the engine, cut a U-turn in the middle of the street, and roared away as Mom walked around the corner, hot, tired, and cranky.

14
Grandma's

"Al was here, wasn't he?" Mom demanded as soon as she came through the door.

This was Dad's problem, not mine. Let him handle it.

I went out to the backyard and stayed there until Mom called me in for supper. By then they'd reached some decisions on how our family would behave. We would go to church together regularly. Dad would immediately start looking for a job. And he would dump the outlaws from his past — Mike, Jerry, and most of all, Uncle Al.

"I guess I'll have to make a new set of friends," Dad said forlornly. I knew what he meant.

Mom rolled her eyes. "Grow up."

I chose that moment to ask if I could spend the weekend at Grandma's. Mom said "Yes!" immediately.

I got the feeling they needed a weekend alone as much as I did.

On Friday evening Grandpa Hank came to pick me up. He was the only one in the family with a vehicle besides Uncle Al. Hank noticed everything on the way there: who had just painted their house, who had put up a new fence, what kinds of flowers and vegetables were doing well in this dry season, how high the crops were.

"You're just like Dad," I said. "He sees all sorts of things that nobody else bothers about. Then he draws them. Do you draw, too?"

Hank laughed. "Nope. Never had time. I went to work when I was sixteen in a sawmill. Never had a day off since."

I rolled down the car window. Summer-type smells flowed in. I saw a girl my age riding a horse along the fence line, her black-and-white collie dog trotting along behind. I smiled, and she waved.

"Grandma's looking forward to your help with the garden," Hank said. "Those beans are getting ahead of her. Gotta tie them up. And there's a bit of weeding to be done. Do you mind?"

"No, I sure don't," I said, and I meant it. Grandma and Hank lived such different lives from Mom and Dad. Or Gemma, or Uncle Al. It was as if we were all from different families.

"Al's coming for supper tomorrow night," Hank said suddenly.

"Oh, how come?"

"He likely plans to ask your Grandma for money again."

"Why? Isn't Uncle Al rich?"

"Rich? That man hasn't a pot to pee in, or a window to throw it out of."

I burst out laughing. "Well, he *looks* rich."

"That's why he ain't," Hank said. "It's all show and nothing underneath. I hope your daddy has the sense that God gave a goose and stays away from him. That Al will get him into trouble again, sure as shootin'."

"I'll help. If he comes to our house again, I'll tell Mom. She'll chase him away."

"*Again?*" Hank stared at me quizzically.

"I mean, since Dad got home this time."

"Yeah, I bet she'd chase him away — right into the next county! She's got strength of character. I always did like your mom. She's a lot like your grandma. She's more like her than either of her own kids."

When we pulled into the driveway, Grandma came out to meet us, as she always did. Everything with Grandma started and ended with a big hug. "Angel, you're going to be *our* girl for a whole weekend," she said with a big smile. "We'll think of lovely things to do."

In minutes I was in another world. I was eating fresh raspberries off prickly bushes, and peas and baby carrots. Nobody minded how many I picked as long as I didn't waste them. Grandma had two cats, Molly and Missy, and an old dog named Trixie who, for most of the late spring and summer, lived in the holes she'd dug for herself under the house. It was cool and private. I crawled under there, but I got scared of the spiders hanging above me, and freaked out by nets of webs choked with dust and dead flies.

"Can we have organic vegetables for supper?" I asked, and Grandma and Hank laughed.

"Everything here is *organic*," Hank said.

I blushed. Of course, it was. They'd never spray their food with chemicals.

On Saturday evening we got ready for our guest. I'd placed a jar of flowers in the centre of the table: daisies, baby's breath, and forget-me-nots. Grandma's best china was laid out.

"I got that set from buying at the same grocery store every week for three years," she said proudly. "You could get a plate, or a cup and saucer, with each fifty dollars' worth of grub. Lordy, I was scared they'd cut the program before I got my set of eight."

"It's pretty," I said, admiring the pink roses on my plate.

"It'll be yours when I'm done with it," she said. "You appreciate quality. Gemma doesn't care about that. She's too busy painting her face."

The roar of a car engine resounded through the quiet street, and a cloud of dust told us that our dinner guest had arrived. Uncle Al pulled into the yard and then sat inside the car until the dust settled. He opened the door, got out, shook out the cuffs of his light tan-coloured pants, adjusted his tie, straightened the lapels of his sports coat, and strolled in.

Uncle Al's shoulders filled the doorway. His black hair and moustache made him look like a movie star, and he knew it. He stood in a pose, then grabbed Grandma in a hug. "How are ya, sister-in-law?" He formally shook Hank's hand. "Nice to see ya, Hank!" He gave my ponytail a tug. "How are ya, kid?"

He'd brought gifts — a crystal vase for Grandma, which he put my flowers into and threw the old jar out the door — and a pouch of pipe tobacco for Hank. "High class stuff!" Uncle Al announced in case Hank hadn't noticed the brand.

For me he'd brought a beautiful bracelet of pink rhinestones alternating with clear diamond-like stones all the way around that fastened with a little clip. "It's called a tennis bracelet," he said. "Picked it up for you at the club."

What?

"Oh, my," said Grandma as she stood back to admire the flowers in their beautiful vase.

"Well, well," said Hank as he carefully put the tobacco away in a drawer. "I'll have to save this for special occasions."

I'd never owned anything as beautiful as this bracelet. "Thank you," I managed to say. I asked Uncle Al to help fasten it on my wrist.

"You're just as beautiful as that bracelet," Uncle Al said. "Count on it, Angela Wroboski will be breaking hearts."

Supper was wonderful. Grandma had cooked a roast with gravy, new potatoes, fresh peas and little carrots, tomato-and-lettuce salad, all from the garden. For dessert we had rhubarb-and-strawberry pie with real whipped cream.

Uncle Al kept us laughing throughout the meal. I glanced over at Hank. Although he was laughing, too, I thought of what he'd said. Was Hank right that Uncle Al was coming to try to borrow money from Grandma? But how could he buy all these lovely presents if he was broke?

Grandma and I cleared the table but left the dishes until later. Grandma was like that. She didn't break the fun just to do work. "We'll do them when it's cooler, after Al's gone," she said. That was fine with me.

We sat out on the front verandah as everyone did in the evenings here when the weather was good. In many ways this was a much better place to live than the city.

Uncle Al sat on the railing of the verandah, chatting with Hank. They discussed the government, the weather, the crops, and Hank's job.

"And how's your business going, Al?" Hank said, with a wink at me.

I knew I'd better listen.

"Actually, that's what I came to talk to you about," Uncle Al said smoothly. "I'm on the verge of making it big. *Real* big. I've got steady, good-paying contracts, more business than I'd ever expected. But I'm gonna have to expand if I want to stay on top. I need another car and driver."

Hank, Grandma, and I stared straight ahead.

"I'm thinking of taking Nick into the business."

"*What!*" Hank, Grandma, and I all said at once.

"Well, yeah, the little fella has had a rough time lately," Uncle Al said. "What kind of job can he get? Grade ten education, a prison record. Who's going to hire him?"

"The city!" I said. "He's going back digging graves."

"Honey, I hate to tell you this, but things have changed since your daddy had that job. City employees are in a union now. If you're not in the union, they won't hire you. And they don't dig graves with shovels anymore. Their men operate big machines, do ten graves at once, put a lid on 'em till they're needed. Who's going to hire Nick to operate a backhoe or a grader or a 'dozer? Those are hundred-thousand-dollar machines!"

We sat back. I felt frightened — for Dad and for our family. The future suddenly seemed so hopeless.

"So like I was saying," Uncle Al continued, "Nicky needs a break. I won't take him in as a full partner, of course. He's got to come up with some dough if he wants to become part owner. I sure didn't get anything handed to me."

"I lent you the money for that old Cadillac, that big limo you're driving right now," Grandma said. "You haven't paid it all back yet. You still owe me over a thousand dollars."

"I know, and I'll pay the balance real soon. But Nicky needs help. If I could get another car — and it doesn't need to be as good a car as this one, maybe a Chevy or a Ford — then Nicky could be working tomorrow."

"How, when he hasn't got a driver's licence?" Grandma said.

Uncle Al flicked his cigarette butt over the side of the railing onto Grandma's flower bed below. "That's just paperwork. I can look after that."

"Don't you get him driving with a fake licence!" Grandma said. "He'll get caught — he always does — and then he'll be back in the hoosegow for good. They'll lock him up and throw away the key."

I'd never heard the term *hoosegow*, but I knew it must mean *jail*. My stomach muscles tightened. Then my eyes started to water. I couldn't help it.

"Why, Angel honey, whatever's the matter?" Grandma jumped up and came over to my chair. She scooped me into her big arms. "*Shhh*, baby, *shhh*, baby," she murmured. Grandma hugged me and patted my hair. "This has been so hard on her. She's just a little girl who loves her daddy."

"I'll teach Nick how to drive," Hank said suddenly. "He'll get his driver's licence the proper way."

"Good," Uncle Al said. "I'd help, but I've got a business to run. I don't seem to have any free time at all anymore. I could sure use Nick. So how about the loan?"

I was still being held by Grandma when she said to Uncle Al, "Look, you need money to get a car so you can hire Nicky, you go to a bank. You've got a business — go get a business loan. When Nicky has a real driver's licence, not some paper that you cooked up, maybe we'll see about helping him with a car. But he gets into trouble dealing with you every time."

"Hey, that was before! I'm on the right side of the law now." Uncle Al stepped down from his seat on the verandah railing. "You think it over while we see what other jobs Nick can get. My bet is he'll be begging to come to work for me. I'll be happy to take him on, but I'll need a little family assistance myself."

Uncle Al's voice sounded smooth like a lullaby. My tears dried. What a good thing that our family helped each other. Maybe Grandma was being too hard on Uncle Al. I decided not to tell her that he had been coming around when Mom was at work.

"He's upset with me," Grandma told us after Uncle Al said goodbye and headed to his car, "and he'll find some way to get even. Maybe I should have just given him the money. That Cadillac's fifteen years old. He got it for a song, but it can't last forever. Maybe he does need another car."

Hank patted her on the shoulder. "No, you did the right thing. You're the first person I've ever seen stand up to Al. Maybe this family is finally getting smart."

Hank, Grandma, and I stood on the porch and watched Uncle Al talk on his cellphone as he backed down the dusty driveway onto the main road. Then he stepped on the gas, and pretty soon all we could see was a puff of dust as the black Cadillac disappeared toward the lights of the city.

15
Beets

On Sunday, Grandma, Hank, and I met Mom and Dad at church. *All right!* After the service, Hank treated us to lunch at a restaurant, and Dad announced that he had a surprise. He'd found a job!

"I saw this ad tacked up in the lobby of the Winchester Hotel," he said, "so I phoned the guy and he hired me just like that!"

"What's the job?" I asked. I noticed that Mom wasn't saying anything, and her face didn't reveal any excitement about this news.

"Well, it's not much, but it's a start," Dad said. "It'll get me back in shape. I need to be out in the sun more, anyway."

"What's the job?" Grandma asked.

"The pay's not too good, but if I put in lots of hours, I should be able to rake in some dough," Dad said.

"*What's the job?*" I asked for the second time.

"Hoeing sugar beets," Dad said.

We'd all seen the beet fields — rows and rows stretching for mile after mile. And we'd seen people working in the fields, backs bent in the hot sun, the wind blowing dust all over. Many families came from far away, even from other countries, and so the farmers provided them with little cabins to live in for the season. When their work here was done, they went back home. Others, hired locally, got a ride to the fields on a special bus.

"I have to be in front of the hotel at five o'clock tomorrow morning," Dad said. "Guy picks us up, takes us out to the field."

I didn't hear Dad leave Monday morning. The next time I saw him he was in the hospital. When he could talk, he told us the story. I later typed it out on Ryan's computer and then printed it for a keepsake, so I would never forget how hard Dad had tried and how difficult it was for him to get a break.

THE BEETS

Dad stands in front of the hotel, waiting for the ride. The sun is up, the sky is pink, and he feels pretty good. Other men are also waiting for the van. Some are wandering labourers who follow crops being harvested, but most are First Nations men from the nearby reserve. Dad has met one of them before, a big guy named Gerald Crow. Gerald nods and moves over to stand beside Dad.

"Got a smoke on you?"

"Yeah, sure." Dad takes a pack from his pocket.

"Thanks." Gerald lights up. "You know these guys don't pay us until the end of the week. They figure we won't come back if we're paid at the end of the shift." Gerald blows out smoke. "They're right," he adds with a crooked smile.

Dad says nothing.

"You ever worked the beets?" Gerald asks.

"Nope."

"Then you've got a lesson coming."

The van arrives, and the men pile in, sitting on benches along the sides.

The minute they arrive at the field the fore-man treats them like slaves. "Okay, let's move it!" he shouts. He sticks a hoe into Dad's hand.

Dad follows Gerald. The heavy green foliage of the beet plants sprout above their large white turnip-like roots. The plants sit solidly in the hard-packed earth like squat little kings. Weeds have to be hoed out and smaller plants thinned. Flies and bees buzz around, especially as the sun climbs into the sky.

"There's a way to do this," Gerald says. "Watch."

He bends at an angle, swinging the narrow hoe down a row, striking out weeds by their roots, moving easily to thin and hoe, thin and hoe.

"You've got to get in stride," Gerald says. "Don't go too fast."

Dad starts hacking around his first beet. His hoe doesn't move smoothly like Gerald's. It digs deep at the weeds, and his movements are choppy. The sun crawls over the eastern horizon. It must be just after six in the morning. Normal people are still sleeping. He thinks of his family still asleep. He slashes quickly, carelessly, trying to catch up to Gerald.

"What the heck do you think you're doing?" The foreman strides up, his eyes angry. He grabs Dad's hoe and swings it in expert arcs. "This is how you go, like *this*! And where's your hat? I suppose you didn't bring one. You'll be fainting by noon." He glances at Dad's black high-top running shoes, his black jeans and open shirt. A look of disgust comes over his face. "I'll be carrying you out of here tonight in a basket." He spits into the dust.

Dad bends again, *swing, chop, swing, chop*, looking only at the beet plant in front of him. By ten o'clock he is wringing wet with sweat and has a sharp pain across his shoulders. Sweat streaks his face and runs into his eyes. His hands are blistered and starting to bleed because he hasn't thought to bring gloves. A blister has bubbled up on his heel from his thin socks rubbing inside his shoes.

A truck horn sounds, and the men walk to the side of the field where the driver gives them coffee. But Dad just wants water. He gulps three cups full.

"You'll kill your stupid self!" the foreman yells. "You don't down water quick like that!"

When Dad tells this part, I feel so sad. I brush his bandaged hand. Poor Dad — doesn't even know how to drink water correctly.

He trudges back to his place on the beet row.

Noon. His lunch is now a flattened warm slab. The white bread has turned yellow from mustard, and his baloney slice looks slightly green. He eats it, anyway.

Gerald comes up to him. "Nick, I've got to tell you something. You're not going to last. Take my advice. Go slowly. Move just enough so the foreman knows you're alive. Then at home tonight, rub yourself down with liniment. Tomorrow, if you can get out of bed, wear loose canvas shoes, gloves, and a hat."

"How come you don't need a hat?" Dad asks.

Gerald laughs. "Hey, we were under this sun long before these guys came and planted their little beets." He stands. "Well, back to it."

Gerald says Dad could do nearly an acre a day if he was in shape, but most people do a half-acre. And they're paid by the acre.

"I thought we'd be paid by the hour," Dad says.

"No, no. This way, if you take a break, they don't have to pay you for it."

Dad starts hoeing again, but the pain in his shoulders and back is so intense that he can't straighten up anymore. They take another break at three o'clock in the afternoon. Two more hours to work before the foreman blows the whistle. An eleven-hour workday! In over thirty degrees Celsius!

By four o'clock, Dad can no longer straighten his back, and his arms feel as if they've doubled in length. His feet are curled up in his shoes to prevent the blisters from rubbing. His head is splitting, and strange images start to swim in front of his eyes. He can barely see the plants.

Dad grabs the hoe, bends to make a stroke, and everything turns black. He wakes up on the ground in the shade of the van with Gerald staring down at him.

"Good, you're alive," Gerald says. "I thought you were done for. You're burning up. Look, you're not even sweating anymore."

Dad's skin is warm and dry like a rattlesnake's. His head throbs until he thinks his skull will burst. He tries to raise his head, but his vision swirls, and he falls back onto the dusty ground.

"Just lie still," Gerald says. "We're leaving in a minute. We've got to get you to a hospital."

"No!" Dad yells, but he feels himself being lifted in Gerald's big arms and propped up on the bench in the van. The men buzz around like bees. Dad thinks he might vomit, and does. The men swear and scream, falling over him to get out.

Dad wakes up in a white room, with Mom and me sitting on each side of his bed. Gerald Crow is standing at the end of the bed like an anxious father.

"Doc said it was the worst case of sunstroke he's ever seen," Gerald says. "Well, pal, guess you're over the worst of it." He nods to Mom and me. "Look after him!" And he's gone.

Dad stays in the hospital for three days, getting over his sunstroke and back muscle spasms.

I visit him every day. So do Mom, Grandma, and Gemma. And so, I find out, do Uncle Al, Mike, and Jerry.

And that was the story of my dad's first job.

16
Sports

The day of my school sports day and picnic the clouds formed black puffs in the sky and rain threatened constantly. But I didn't care. It was cool enough, so I was able to do my best.

I won four firsts, three seconds, and a third. The third was for the relay race, which we should have won, but Hannah dropped the stick just as she was running toward me.

After the race, I looked over and saw she was crying. I wanted to give her a blast. I hate losing. But Mrs. Marsden trotted over to comfort her, saying, "It's all right. Don't worry. It's only a race."

I saw someone else coming toward us, too — Hannah's mother. And walking beside her was my dad.

My heart pounded. I turned away and ran to the far side of the field to wait until the ribbons were handed out.

I'd always known Hannah's family was rich and her dad was a bank manager. She knew we weren't rich but that didn't seem to matter before. To me it wasn't important who our dads were or what they did. It wasn't the kids' fault if their parents weren't perfect. But families of bankers and thieves didn't mix, apparently.

As I walked onto the raised platform to get my track ribbons, Dad and Mrs. Singer were edging through the crowd toward me. I couldn't believe they'd gotten together.

Hannah sidled up to me on the platform. I wouldn't look at her.

"My mom and your dad have met," she said. "Maybe they'll like each other and everything will be okay."

I stared straight ahead.

"They must have met while they were watching the relay race," Hannah said.

"Good. I hope they saw what you did."

She was silent for a moment. I felt awful.

Later I discovered Dad and Mrs. Singer had started talking about art. Dad had said he loved the necklace she'd made that Hannah had given me for my birthday. He'd even asked her to come to our house to see his artwork sometime.

"You didn't tell me your dad was an artist," Hannah said.

"Since when did you care about *con artists*?" I said sarcastically.

I wished that a big mine shaft would suddenly cave in and I'd drop down like Alice in Wonderland. Except the world above ground was weirder than Wonderland.

Dad took a couple of weeks off to rest up after his sugar beet job. By then it was into July. He told Mom he wanted to stay home and look after me now that school was out and I'd be "on the loose" all day. What a laugh.

I generally got up around nine o'clock, made my breakfast, did the dishes, and tidied up the house. Dad slept until noon. When he did get up, he made a big mess, so I did housework twice. In the afternoon I usually went over to Ryan's house for a couple of hours and we played games on the computer. It was fun. His mom was glad he'd finally found a normal friend.

One morning I was leaving for Ryan's when Dad asked if I could press his good pants and a white shirt.

"I'm checking out the Employment Centre," he announced.

"Can I come with you?" I asked, intrigued.

"What for?"

"Why not?" Actually, I had a feeling he might need some guidance.

"Well, okay."

We walked down the street together. I'd gotten used to the way Dad looked, but I forgot how other people regarded him. His hair had grown out some and he brushed it back, but it was still in between any kind of style. I asked him why he'd had it cut so short in the first place. "I liked it that way. Clean-cut, like me."

He always had a cigarette going. In the long-sleeved shirt he was wearing today, you couldn't see his tattoos, but his tie was out-of-date. It didn't seem right — nothing like the type Hannah's father wore. His black pants were okay. He wanted to wear his black boots with the chains, but I said, "No, you should wear dress shoes," so he did to please me. Dad hadn't worn them for two years, and by the way he was walking I think they were too tight.

When we got to the office, I went with Dad up to the counter.

"What can I do for you?" the man asked.

"Need a job," Dad said. "Either that or pogey."

"Pogey?" I said.

"EI."

"Employment insurance," the man explained for my benefit. Then he asked Dad, "You got a claim?"

"Huh?"

The man sighed. "You work, you build up weeks. When you're out of a job, you get a record of employment stating how long you worked and why you aren't there anymore, whether you were laid off, or fired, or quit. You bring that form in here and file your claim. You get benefits while you look for a new job."

"Well, I ain't had work. That's why I need these benefits right now."

"Where was your last job?"

"Hoeing beets."

"For how long?"

"One day."

"That all?"

"Yeah."

"I mean, is that the only place you've worked in the past year?"

"That's about it."

"Education? Training?"

Dad shrugged. "Finished grade ten, is all. Then did odd jobs."

"The only job we've got for a man with not much education or job skills is at the packing plant on the kill floor. You want to see about it?"

"Never!" Dad slapped his hand on the counter.

The man frowned. "Fine, I can't force you. Go find something better yourself."

Dad grabbed my arm. "Come on. We're going to City Hall."

I sniffed the air like a society lady and accompanied Dad down the stairs and out to the street. "What's at City Hall, Dad? Do you have an appointment with the mayor?"

He smiled. "No, we won't exactly be going to the City Hall downtown. We'll go to city's public works yard. I got an in there, fella who knows me. I'll get my old job back before you can say 'Bob's your uncle.'"

It took us a half-hour to walk. I didn't mind. We went slowly, but Dad was limping pretty badly by the time we got there.

"I wanna see the foreman," Dad said. "I worked here before. Tell him Nick Wroboski's back."

I wondered if anybody here would really care. It wasn't as if he was a celebrity or anything.

In a few minutes a man came out of a back room. He took a package of tobacco out of his shirt pocket along with some cigarette papers and hand-rolled a smoke. "I don't remember you," he said as he licked the paper and closed it, "and I've been here seventeen years. Don't recall your name at all."

"I dug graves," Dad said. "Six months. I ... I liked it here. It was a real good job."

My heart lurched.

The foreman arched an eyebrow. "Yeah? Who you work with?"

"Guy named Willie Frank."

"That thief!" the foreman snapped. "I run him off. Caught him stealing parts from the shop. You got anyone *else* who can vouch for you?"

"He's the only one I got to know real well. I'd come in, get the map, be told where to dig the grave, and I'd go dig it."

"We use backhoes now. Excavators. You run one of them?"

"Huh?"

"Backhoes, man! The machine out there." We walked outside, and he pointed at a yellow tractor with a scoop on one end. "Those things. You run one?"

"Nope."

"No? You just worked with a shovel and pick? That must have taken forever. The city's growing — got no time for custom-made graves. We can do a dozen graves a day with this equipment."

Dad squinted up at the foreman. The sun was in his eyes, and he blinked like a mole. "You need that many graves now? Someone killing off our citizens?"

His attempt to make a joke fell flat, and I felt scared and kind of ashamed again — and also ashamed of feeling ashamed. I was so mixed up. Why couldn't we have a normal family like Hannah's? A dad who worked, a mom who volunteered on committees, brothers who studied with plans to go to university, all living in a big comfy house?

"The ground's *frozen* in the winter," the foreman said in reply to Dad's goofy comment, "so we get ahead of the orders when the ground's soft. Well, we can't use you if you don't know how to operate heavy equipment."

"How do I learn?"

"You also gotta be in the union."

"Union?"

"Yeah, union. Nupee."

"What?"

The foreman looked as if he had a pain. "National Union of Public Employees — NUPE!"

"Oh."

"Well, look, you go somewhere, learn how to operate equipment, or take an air brakes course, something useful, and then come back. We'll test you out. If you're any good, we can apply to get you permitted by the union. Where was your last full-time job?"

"Here."

"Here?" The foreman took off his cap and scratched his head. "When did you say that was?"

"Four years ago."

"And you haven't worked since?"

"Nope ... I been away."

"Did you work somewhere else? *Away?*"

"Yeah, but not paid work."

The foreman glanced at me, then leaned over to Dad, giving him a hard look. "You been in jail?" he whispered.

"Jail? Oh, no! I just been ... travelling. Worked down east for a while."

"What doing?"

"With horses. At the track."

"Well, that won't get you much of a reference. Take a course or something. You got your grade twelve?"

"Nope."

"Eleven? You can take a machine-operating course with grade eleven."

"Nope."

The foreman barked an order at one of the men, then turned back to us. "Well, I gotta go. You think about it. Only place you can get a job anymore, without much training or education, is at the packing plant. You try there?"

"Not yet," Dad said.

"My wife's brother works there, but he's quitting. Go ask about his old job. He's a liver-spiker."

Dad grabbed my hand, and we turned to leave. Behind us the backhoe started up, its motor vibrating.

The operator sat in the seat and then expertly moved the machine ahead. Dad followed it with his eyes.

"Yeah, I'll go see about that job," Dad said. "Thanks."

We walked across the public works yard and back onto the street.

"A liver-spiker!" I said. "Is that what I *think* it is?"

"I don't know," Dad said.

We walked along in silence.

"There's gotta be something I can do," he said quietly. "Someone, somewhere, must need a good man."

17
Education

I felt angry at what was going on around this place. Just after Mom left for work the phone would ring and Dad would hurry to answer it. A short while later Uncle Al would show up, often with Mike and Jerry.

Sometimes they had coffee here and talked in low voices around the kitchen table. But sometimes they went outside to the backyard and sat at our old wooden picnic table, which Dad had moved under a tree at the far end of the yard so I couldn't hear their conversations anymore.

Other times Dad waited for Uncle Al outside at the curb and jumped in as the big black car slowed to a stop. When Dad went away with Uncle Al, he didn't return until about an hour before Mom was due home from the office. Then he'd flick on the TV and watch old crime shows or cartoons.

At first I thought Uncle Al was taking him out to Grandpa Hank's for some driving lessons until Hank called and asked when Dad wanted to start. I had brought a driver's manual home, but Dad hadn't opened it.

I liked my Uncle Al, even though I felt nervous being around him. He was so powerful.

When he saw all the Sports Day ribbons I'd won, he said, "Congratulations, kid!" Then he counted out a ten-dollar bill for each first, five dollars for each second, and two dollars for each third. "And here's more for being a good kid." He slapped a twenty into my hand. "Don't spend it all in one place."

"Thank you. This is a lot of money."

He laughed. "Get used to it, kid. There's more where that came from. Lots more."

Uncle Al wanted to help us. I knew that. Just yesterday he had taken me aside and told me about a job for Dad.

"It's on a ranch, the Flying Bee," he'd said. "That kind of work doesn't require a man with much education — just a strong back. Friend of mine told me about it. Tell your Mom, but don't bother saying the tip came from me."

So I made up another story. Uncle Al had pulled me into his scene just as he had everyone else who came in contact with him. In school we had studied things like approach-avoidance conflicts where you were pulled between wanting to do something and not wanting to do it. We also learned about love-hate relationships. I was in one now. So I lied to Mom, truly believing it was for the good of the family.

"Mom, I saw a job on the bulletin board at the grocery store," I said casually as Mom and I did the dishes together. "Maybe Dad would like it — working on a ranch."

"Your father's lost his confidence," Mom said in a low voice so Dad couldn't hear. "He's heard no too many times."

I really wanted to be proud of him — he was my dad, after all — but he had to be proud of himself, too. He had to quit being an idiot!

Later I heard Mom telling Dad about the job. "Try for it, Nick," she urged. "It can't hurt. The worst they can do is say no."

"I don't have a way out there," Dad said sullenly. "How am I supposed to get back and forth to a ranch every day? They don't come in with a van like the beet people do."

"Maybe you could stay a few days at a time. They must have a bunkhouse," Mom said. Seeing Dad's gloomy look, she threw down the dish towel and sat wearily on a chair. "Oh, Nick, I don't know. There's got to be something you can do."

"Maybe you could hitchhike out there," I said.

Dad glared at me, but I didn't care.

The ranch was thirteen miles southeast of town. Dad got up early the next morning and stumbled into the shower. Mom and I fixed him a big breakfast and packed his lunch.

He said goodbye like a man going to the electric chair. But in reality all he had to do was walk a few blocks to the highway and stick out his thumb.

After he left, Mom and I sat at the kitchen table.

"I wonder what story we're going to hear when he comes home tonight," Mom said, sighing loudly.

"Maybe he won't be home tonight," I said optimistically. "Maybe they'll put him to work right away and give him a bed in their bunkhouse."

"Maybe."

After Mom left for work, I tidied up the house, but still felt restless when I was finished. I had to talk to somebody. But who? I decided to phone Hannah.

The minute she heard my voice she said, "Oh, Angela, I'm so glad you called. I've missed you! Please come over right away."

"No, I can't right now." How could I face her family? What if her father refused to let me in the house? I was getting as nervous as Dad. "Let's meet in the New Day Café," I suggested. "I'll buy you a sundae. I made some money."

"Lucky you! I've been trying to get babysitting jobs, but there aren't many. Did you find one?"

"No. My uncle gave me some money for winning those sports ribbons. See you in half an hour."

We sat in a back booth. At first we talked about everything except our families — sports day, our school reports, what teachers we'd have next year, and whether there would be any cute boys in our class.

"I hear you've been seeing Ryan Phelps ... going over to his house," Hannah said. "You like him?"

"He's okay. We play games on the Internet, stuff like that."

"Looking up hot celebs' fan pages?"

"No, doing science stuff mostly."

"Sounds boring."

"No, it's pretty fun." I dug into my chocolate fudge sundae as if it were the first thing I'd eaten in days.

"Mom wants to see your dad's art, but my dad won't let her," Hannah said finally.

I poked deeply into the tulip-shaped sundae glass, down where the chocolate lay deep and dark like my mood.

"My dad's known all along about your dad," Hannah said. "He said all bank managers get computer updates on people like him."

I jabbed in the long spoon and scraped it around

the bottom of the glass, making an irritating screeching sound. Hannah winced.

"People like him," I repeated. "Now just what kind of information do you get on *people like him?"*

She shifted in her seat. "Well, you know, about people who rob banks. People with breaking-and-entering records."

"My dad didn't rob banks!" I shouted, causing other diners to stare. I wasn't sure anymore what Dad had really done, but I wasn't taking this kind of crap from her or anyone else. I might be secretly frightened and a bit ashamed at times, but Hannah was an outsider — a double outsider with her banking father — and this was strictly family business. "Anyway, that's private information," I snapped.

"Not really. Lots of people know. Banks, police, social workers, teachers ..."

"Teachers?"

"You think Mrs. Madsen didn't know what you were going through? Why she gave you a passing mark in math?"

"I passed *fairly.*"

She leaned across the table. "Angela, it's *okay.* Don't be so defensive. Nobody blames you for what your dad does, or your uncle, or —"

"My *uncle*! He's never done anything!"

"Well, he's never been *caught.* Dad says he's just

125

lucky because he's behind most of it."

"He knows my Uncle Al?"

"Everyone knows him. He looks like a mobster, and he drives that big black Cadillac with those pink letters on it — Dial-a-Dream! Everyone's scared of him. They say he packs a gun."

Okay, should I slide down in my seat and hide, or should I blast her and make a real scene?

Neither. I took a deep breath.

"My family's had some problems, but we're doing okay. My dad paid for his mistake. Now he wants to put it behind him and go straight. He's starting a new job today, in fact."

"Doing what?" Hannah asked.

It was really none of her business, but I decided to try to give her a better impression. "He's working on a big ranch, just for now, to get in shape." Then before I could think about it I blurted, "In the fall he's going back to school."

"How can he? He's too old!"

"He's enrolling in computer school. He's looking into buying a good computer with a high-end graphics card. And he's learning to drive, too!"

"All adults should know how to drive."

"Maybe some never had the chance or wanted to."

"Oh, I suppose so."

"So we're starting now. Dad's going to learn some completely new skills."

"That's nice." Hannah's face was red. She had barely touched her sundae. "You can maybe borrow my brothers' books," she offered. Then, warming up to the idea, she started talking and eating at the same time until ice cream and words were both dripping from her lips. "Josh got top marks in grade eight math and science. He kept all his notes. Andrew just passed grade ten with honours! He's got lots of computer books. When you get your own computer, I can burn you a CD with his stuff on it."

"Thanks. But isn't that illegal?"

She giggled. "I don't know. Is it? We download and burn music onto discs all the time. It can't be any different. It's not like it's a program — it's his work! I'll help you get your dad back into the business world, too."

We gave each other chocolate smiles across the table.

18
Skunks

Dad came home late. Rather, someone dumped him off at the curb around ten o'clock at night.

When he entered the house, he looked homeless and smelled worse. Mom and I helped him to a kitchen chair. His hair was messed, and he was covered with a coating of chaff from hay or grain. He was sneezing with an attack of hay fever, and his eyes were red and watering. His shirt was torn and dirty, and his pants had to be thrown out. Worse, he absolutely *reeked* of skunk. But it was the pathetic, beaten look on his face that was hardest to take.

I ran to fill the bathtub with warm water, adding bubble bath, while Mom punched open a can of tomato juice.

"Here, go into the bathroom, take off your clothes, and rub this juice over yourself," she said. "It'll help to take away the skunk smell."

He dutifully shuffled into the bathroom. We heard him thumping around as he shed his clothes. Mom went in and returned with the clothes in a bundle. She shoved them into a garbage bag and took them outside.

Soon Dad was back, wearing a clean T-shirt and jeans. The smell was almost gone.

"Okay, tell us what happened," Mom said. Her voice was low and smooth as if she were coaxing a little animal from its burrow.

Dad got a beer from the fridge and took a deep swallow. "Morning starts good. The air's full of birds, telephone wires are singing away. I feel good. I get a ride real quick, nice guy, a salesman. He drops me off, and I walk a couple miles in. No sweat." He took a sip of beer.

We waited, wondering how and when this happy story would go bad.

"So I go along till I see the sign FLYING BEE RANCH. I turn in at the gate and walk up the longest driveway in the world. A woman's standing at the door of the house, shaking a rug.

"'Hey, lady,' I say. 'I'm looking for a job. Foreman around?' 'My husband's over by the machine shed,' she says, and points. I go over there. A big black dog comes out, sniffs me, curls his lip. I don't like dogs, you know that, scared of 'em, but I keep walking and I don't look at him. So I find the foreman. 'Yeah, we got a job,' he says, 'but it don't look to me like you're up to it. You don't look in very good shape.' I say, 'Whaddya mean? I've just been hoeing beets! This job harder than that?' So he hires me."

Mom and I gave a cheer, but Dad shook his head sadly and put up his hand to halt us. The worst was yet to come.

"So the guy, he asks me where's my duffle and sleeping bag. I say, 'Hey, it's nine o'clock in the morning. I ain't going to bed yet!' But he doesn't laugh. He says, 'You're not planning on living in those clothes for a week, are you? You didn't drive in here and you can't walk out at five o'clock. When we're haying, we're haying! All night till the dew comes.' I ask him, 'What's the job?' And he gets real mad. 'You never been on a ranch before? Haying means cutting and baling hay. Horses eat it.' I tell him I know what horses eat. I used to work with horses at the racetrack down east. But he just sneers and says I won't even be *seeing* the horses."

Dad was quiet for a minute. Mom and I waited. My stomach started to cramp.

"The job they get me doing is called *barging*. I have to follow the baler. Behind the baler is a barge, a flat raft thing. I'm supposed to stack these square bales on the barge in a pyramid. When I get eight of 'em stacked up, I take a crowbar and hoist them off, so *they fall stacked*."

He bangs his beer bottle on the table. "It would take a *magician* to do that!"

Dad looked around for our sympathy. Mom and I nodded.

"You've got to have *perfect* coordination," Dad said. "You've got to get the bales off right or they fall all over the place. My crowbar got stuck in the slats of the barge. I'd have to run along behind and get it, then catch up. And meanwhile bales are tossing around like popcorn. I'm sneezing and coughing from the seeds, pollen, chaff, eyes watering, can't see." He stopped talking for a moment. "And then it happened."

All breathing stopped. My stomach gave a violent lurch, and I leaned forward in my chair, listening intently, not wanting to miss a word. Sweat misted Dad's forehead, and I thought he might faint.

Finally, Mom asked gently, "You want to tell us, Nick?"

Dad ripped the label off his beer bottle until it was peeled down in three even strips. "It was the little animals. The little skunks."

"Oh, no!" Mom and I cried.

"The baler picked up a family of skunks. They went right through. Couldn't do a thing about it." Dad glanced up at us, his face haggard. "I could have *bawled*. Right there. Big tough man, eh?"

I moved over to Dad and gave him a hug. He smelled fairly good now, of my bubble bath. The skunk smell was just a faint memory. We sat there, Mom beside him at the table patting his shoulder, Dad with his arm around me.

"I've got an idea, Dad. No more stupid jobs. Ryan and I are going to teach you everything you need to know about computers over the summer. He has all sorts of software programs, and you can enroll in a course in the fall."

"Computers? Me?"

Mom laughed. "Yeah, right."

Dad laughed, too, but there was a small look of hope, even of interest, on his face. An expression that hadn't been there when he walked through the door an hour ago, reeking like a skunk and hanging his head like a sad dog.

19
Poker Patience

July passed slowly: some babysitting jobs, hanging out in the backyard, reading, meeting Hannah at the New Day Café or for an afternoon at the swimming pool, and going over to Ryan's. One day Dad came home with a laptop computer. "Borrowed it from a friend," he said, and neither Mom nor I asked anything further. We had to get a computer sooner or later. Ryan offered to come over and help set up an email account and download some programs. He was excited at the idea of being Dad's tutor. He okayed it with his mother, and the next day he arrived.

"You'll be starting with Microsoft Office Professional, Mr. Wroboski," Ryan said. Dad looked blank. "Then we'll go online on the Net ..." He began again. "I'll show you what a computer *can do*, Mr. Wroboski."

When Dad seemed to start grasping the purposes of a computer, Ryan said, "Hey, you'll be surfing the Net in no time, Mr. Wroboski, and communicating with everyone in the world who shares your same interests! I mean, you'll learn all sorts of new things …"

"Yes, Professor!" Dad said, smiling. As the hours jumped along, Ryan explained about email messaging, how to send and receive, and together they explored the World Wide Web.

"I've always been excited about multimedia, Mr. Wroboski," Ryan said. "We can package several modules for a single course that teaches multiple applications for a microcomputer."

"Sure."

"What would you like to learn, basically?"

"He wants to know how to do business stuff," I said. "His uncle is thinking of making him a partner someday."

"Fine, then. We'll do multimedia tasking and then some hands-on exercises. You'll learn by doing."

After three hours, I could see Dad's attention begin to flag. I didn't blame him. He'd gone from labouring jobs to high-tech and into a world where nobody cared what you looked like, what grade you got to in school, or what secrets you had in your past life.

"See, Dad, it's all in the way you work your mouse!" I said as Dad clicked his way through cyberspace.

Dad laughed. "Okay if this cat comes back tomorrow? I like the way he explains things."

Ryan and I smiled at each other. Dad noticed our expressions and chuckled.

Sometime later I found out that Dad was a math whiz.

"Where did you learn?" I asked him after Ryan returned home following another lesson.

"Cards," Dad replied. He grabbed a deck of playing cards from the table and began to shuffle them so quickly the cards blurred. "Poker patience. Watch. You lay all the cards in five rows, five cards each. See? Five up and down, five across. Get it?"

"Yeah."

"The best poker hand, the one that gives you the best score, is a straight flush."

"What's that?"

"Try to get five cards in the same suit — hearts, diamonds, spades, or clubs, one number after another." He spread out a six, seven, eight, nine, and ten of hearts. "But the very best is a royal straight flush, using ace, king, queen, jack, and ten."

"Okay." But I was quickly losing interest.

"Wanna have a game?"

"No, not really."

"Aw." He set the cards down, lit up a smoke, and flicked on the TV to watch cartoons.

At six o'clock Gemma arrived after her shift at the store. Little barrettes were tucked into her hair. She pulled off a pair of rhinestone-trimmed sunglasses and placed them on top of her head. Gemma was wearing lots of black mascara on both upper and lower lashes, tons of light pink lip gloss, and Barbie-pink polish on both fingers and toes. A slightly see-through white tank top, tight, low-waisted jeans, a big-buckled white leather belt, and opalescent white flip-flops completed her ensemble, along with a little pink purse. As usual she was chewing gum, snapping it for sentence punctuation.

"Hiya, sweetie!" she said. *Snap. Snap.* "Got a cold one for a tired but gorgeous auntie?" *Snap.*

I never thought of Gemma as my "auntie." She was too young and wild. But I guess she was as normal as anyone in this family. And she had a job — fairly rare around here.

Dad grabbed the remote, flicked off the TV, and waved his hand toward the fridge. "Help yourself."

Gemma grabbed a Coke and slumped into a chair, kicking off her flip-flops and spreading out her toes. The nails sparkled in the light.

"Purr-fectly Pink, it's the new 'shimmer' line," she said, seeing my look. "My lip gloss matches. Like it?"

Gemma's blond hair was styled all curly and pulled up on her head with little diamond barrettes. Her dark roots were growing in.

"Yeah. It looks good on you."

Gemma turned to Dad. "How come Uncle Al doesn't come around anymore? Jerry says this place has been declared off-limits."

Dad looked away. "I haven't had time to see people much."

"Your *probation officer* tell you to stop?" she said, gesturing at me.

"Angela's no probation officer! She's helping me study. I'm learning to use the computer, right, Angela?"

I smiled. "Right."

"Yeah, yeah." Gemma laughed and punched Dad on the shoulder. "What about Uncle Al? He help you find work yet?"

There seemed to be a veiled message in her question. Aunt Gemma knew more than she was letting on.

"Aw, you know Connie doesn't like him. I'll have to tell Uncle Al to find a new partner for Dial-a-Dream. He'll be pretty burned."

I pretended I was listening to my MP3 player I'd gotten last Christmas from my American grandmother. Ryan and Hannah had uploaded the music onto it from their computers for me before we had our own.

137

I turned the music really low, so I could listen to their conversation.

"Con should be happy with you studying and going out every day looking for work," Gemma said.

"Yeah. She is, I guess."

"I saw you down at the bank on Tuesday. I waved, but you didn't see me. You were over by the bank machines, drawing or writing something in a little book."

Dad glanced up. "Yeah?"

"I was going past and I thought it was you, but I couldn't stop — late for work."

"Couldn't have been me. I don't have a bank account yet." His voice suddenly took on a vibrant tone. "But I might have some money coming in soon."

"Oh, where from?" Gemma asked.

"Government."

"Government? You can't collect employment insurance!"

"Maybe I can."

I took one of the headphones out of my left ear and decided to butt in. "How, Dad? You can't do a claim. The man at the employment office said —"

A cagey look came over Dad's face, one I didn't like very much. "I'll have money coming in, you'll see. My own bank account — maybe even a legit credit card."

Gemma seemed satisfied. "Good. Then you can throw a party."

Dad was happy then. "I'll buy champagne, Gemma! Pink champagne!"

She laughed. "Yeah, pink champagne to match my Purr-fectly Pink lip gloss!"

Mom chose that moment to come through the door, carrying a bag of groceries. "Who's talking about pink champagne?"

"We're talking about when we're rich," Gemma said.

"Good!" Mom said. "First thing we'll do is buy a car."

"A new SUV — not an old Cadillac like Uncle Al's!" I said excitedly.

Mom stared at me. "When did you see Uncle Al's car?"

I felt my face get red. "When I was out at Grandma and Hank's," I said quickly, noting Dad's relief.

"So how are we going to get rich?" Mom persisted.

"Everyone's going to get good jobs, Mom, and then we're going to save up."

"Good plan," Mom said.

"I can still pull a good job," Dad said, sounding strangely confident.

"Sure, when Dad learns how to operate computer systems, he can learn CAD and do designs."

"CAD?" Dad said.

"Computer-aided design," I said. "They use it to draw plans of buildings and things like that, figure how rooms will look with furniture in them, or with the door over there instead of here."

"Sounds interesting," Dad said. "Where did you learn that stuff?"

"Ryan was talking about it. He plans to teach you. In the fall you can take some courses in AutoCAD or go to art college."

"Right! Now we're talking. I'll be a college grad."

"Nick's an excellent drawer," Gemma said. "See?" She held out her hand, displaying the oriole, opening and closing her fingers to make the bird fly. "Hey, Nick, why don't you try to get a job as a tattoo artist?"

"Sure, that's a good idea!" I said, joining in the positive mood. "You can draw your designs, then scan them onto the computer and print them out on special paper to make stencils."

"I'll do my best for you all, Angel," Dad said, smiling.

I let the talk swarm around me and pretended I was listening to music again. But I wasn't. Even with his expertise in "poker patience," I was wondering just how good a student my dad would be. And if there really was a place in cyberspace where an ex-con could get a break.

20
Bones

Mom and I were sitting across the table from Dad as he sketched our profiles using a charcoal pencil. A clip-on light hung from the cupboard door, shining down on us. It was hot, and I had to keep pulling my legs off the vinyl chairs before they became stuck forever.

"It's okay, Angel," Dad said. "You don't need to sit so still. I know your shape. Shadowing's the main thing." He made bold strokes, outlining our necks, jawlines, noses, lips, the swirls of our long hair. "There, Con, under your chin there's a bit of a shadow. You two have good bones, you know that?"

Mom shifted a bunch of daisies she was holding for the portrait.

"I notice bones," Dad continued. "You can tell where a person is from by their bones. Indian bones, Slavic bones, European bones, they're all different. I studied that in jail."

"*Shhh*," Mom said.

Mom didn't like hearing Dad talk about jail. It didn't bother me anymore. At least not at home.

"Is that why you like drawing skeletons?" I asked.

"Yeah, maybe. Skeletons are just people with the fat all gone. Clean. No shadows."

Dad worked surely, adding texture and shading. I felt happy and relaxed. Dad's low voice was as soothing as the strokes of his charcoal pencil.

"Nick, you have to get work." Mom's voice slashed our dreamy day.

"Aw, Connie, do you have to rag on about it? My young 'professor' comes here twice a week to —"

"Yes, to play games on a computer."

"It's not games, Mom. It's —"

"Games! I heard you talking about these dragon things and medieval creatures. What are you getting into now? Dungeons and Dragons? Won't that be an improvement. Maybe you'll invent a new game. Let's see, how about Isolation and Inmates?"

Mom then shifted into high gear. "I work eight hours a day, five days a week, at an office! You should see how hard everyone works there, showing up every day on time, taking courses to improve their education, working for promotions. Thankful they have a job at all. And here you are sleeping till noon, getting up to drink coffee and watch TV — and then playing *games*!"

Dad put down his drawing pad, went to his trunk, and brought out a pile of paper. The sheets were covered with computer printouts of home designs. "Look, this is what I've been learning. This is our house. This is that warden's office. I did it on computer, that AutoCAD thing. Pretty good, eh?"

I was impressed, but Mom was on a roll. She shuffled through the drawings and then threw them onto the table. "Great! It must have been a fun exercise, but I don't see any money coming from this. You won't take an ordinary job that pays eight or ten bucks an hour. Oh, no! You won't apply at the packing plant where there's union wages. Oh, no! You'd rather play with this stuff!"

I chose that moment to leave the room. Nobody noticed.

Mom was right in a way. Dad could be applying for simple jobs, working at fast-food restaurants or doing cleaning jobs just to make a few dollars while preparing for college. He hadn't even filled out his application for courses yet.

I went onto the computer and printed out information cards that said WILL BABYSIT, then added my phone number.

"Bye," I said. "I'm going over to Ryan's."

On the way I dropped the cards into people's mailboxes on every street.

I had to talk to someone. I couldn't keep all this to myself anymore. It wasn't fair. I thought and I thought until my head ached and I finally made a hard decision. I would "sing."

One Saturday afternoon when Mom had a day off I joined her downstairs in the laundry room. "Mom, I think something bad's going to happen. I tried to get Dad interested in doing things that might lead to a real job, but I think ... well, Uncle Al ..." And I told her everything. Her face became so sad that I wished I hadn't said anything, but it was out now.

"Maybe nothing will happen ..." I finished, and started to leave the room.

"No, Angela, I've known him too long. I love him, but I don't think I can put up with this much longer. This place is like a halfway house and a bad situation for you. Some people grow up, some never do."

Mom said she'd talk to Dad. She wouldn't say that I'd told her anything, but she'd find a way to let him know she was onto him. I felt relieved — but not for long.

When I got up in the morning, Dad was sitting at the kitchen table, drinking a coffee. He didn't glance up when I said good morning.

"You double-crossed me," he said. He was drawing a big yellow canary, using a felt marker to make bold feather strokes.

I felt badly but refused to back down. "Can't you see who's *really* double-crossing you?" I asked. "Can't you see Uncle Al for how he really is?" I started to cry. I couldn't help it. "Don't leave us again, Dad! You'll be caught and you'll go to jail, maybe for years."

Dad listened in stony silence. I poured a glass of juice and tried to drink it, but my throat had closed. I slammed the glass down on the table, spilling some on his open-beak canary picture. Then I left him sitting there. He didn't look up as I turned to close the door.

Dad, Mom, and I formed a silent truce over the next couple of weeks. None of us mentioned the showdown.

I got some babysitting jobs as a result of my cards, one where the family wanted me to come every day for a week. But when I showed up on Friday morning the lady said she had finished her course early. She paid me, and I came home. It was raining and cold, so I hurried down the sidewalk.

The house was empty, but I could tell at a glance what had gone on since I'd left at eight o'clock that morning. Dad had made coffee. There was the cup and spoon. A pack of cigarettes was missing from the top of the fridge. He hadn't eaten. Someone else had also been here — all the kitchen chairs were pulled back and there were too many butts in the ashtray for just Dad. Uncle Al and the outlaws, Mike and Jerry, had been here!

I sat on my bed to consider the situation. What should I do? The stakes were extreme. I could never tell the police what I knew. It might save Dad, but there was an equal chance I'd lose him and my whole family — Grandma, Hank, Gemma — forever. Any more trouble and Mom would definitely kick him out, and likely divorce him, allowing Uncle Al to really get his hooks into him. Telling Grandma and Hank would cause terrible grief. Telling Gemma would be crazy. She'd tell Jerry I was a squealer, and who knew what they'd do? But I had to do something — and quickly. It was so hard being a jailbird's kid. I had to be loyal to the bad people and lie to the good ones, and things got all mixed up.

After I cleaned out Patsy's cage, I decided to hang it in the living room for a change. Then I got a glass of water from the jug in the fridge and went into my bedroom. I was just starting to read a fashion magazine that Gemma had given to me. I flopped down onto my bed with a bag of chips, planning to read and lounge all day and give my brain a rest. Sounded great!

I was learning how to get the Audrey Hepburn look, chic and sheer, that was coming in again, when I heard a key rattle in the back door lock. Instead of getting up to see who it was, I quietly pulled the duvet over my head.

I heard Dad's quick nervous voice as he entered the house, and then another person's, hushed. It was Uncle Al. A heavy object clunked onto the table. Chairs scraped back, then forward. Uncle Al said something in a low tone, and Dad replied, "No way!"

"You're sure no one's here?" Uncle Al asked.

"I *told* you! Con's at work, Angela's babysitting all day."

"Okay." A chair scraped. "You know, I can't believe you botched this job! What route did you take to get back here?"

"I had to hoof it. Jerry was gone. I was on my own. Over to Fourteenth, back through the old brewery yards, circled around. No one saw me. I swear!"

Uncle Al's voice rasped again, like a file against stone. "Listen here, Nick. You've bungled your last job with me. You and I are through! Leaving me to carry it out alone. And I'm firing that stupid Jerry, too. Taking off when he hears a siren — from a *fire truck*!"

"I couldn't let down my wife, my kid," Dad said. "And it was *you* who screwed up big time. Why'd you fire that gun? Where are your brains, man? Now it's armed robbery! That's federal time, man, and I'm not taking it, not this time, not ever again."

Suddenly, Patsy started to sing.

"What's that?" Uncle Al yelled.

"Angela's bird."

"A *canary*?"

"Yeah. Con bought it for her. Angela usually keeps it in her bedroom. Don't know what it's doing out here."

"It's *singing*!" Uncle Al's voice carried a tone I'd never heard before. Fear. "The cops will be all over us!"

Patsy's singing reached a high note, held, and then broke into a series of trills.

"You shot someone, didn't you?" Dad said.

I went cold under my down-filled duvet.

"It was an accident," Uncle Al said. "I don't think I killed him."

I prayed in silence. *Dear God, let this be a bad dream.*

"But I got the dough," Uncle Al said. "And none of it is yours. You didn't *earn* it."

"I know."

"You can't earn a living, straight or crooked."

"I will. Angela's helping me. That's why — that's why I couldn't do it today."

"So you stand by a fifteen-year-old kid and let down the family! I taught you everything, and you let me down."

"Angela's my kid! She has faith in me. She wants to be proud of me. I pull a job and it'll wreck everything. She trusts me ..."

"Save it," Uncle Al barked. "Now I'm a wanted man — thanks to you, *Weasel*. You're good for nothing, you know that?"

The table cracked! I heard a grunt, a slap, and then another followed by a punch. I screamed, but no one heard me over the sound of someone hitting the floor and the loud, manic singing of my canary.

Jumping up, I flung open my door. But I didn't take another step. I was looking down the barrel of a .38 Special.

21
Bird Man

I screamed, and then I must have fainted because I came
to on the floor. Dad was kneeling beside me, and Uncle
Al was staring down.

"Geez, sorry, kid, you nearly bought it," Uncle Al
muttered. He swiped a handkerchief over the blood on
his chin. I wondered where it had come from, and then
recalled the sounds. Dad must have hit Uncle Al!

Dad helped me to a chair. He ran cold water over a
towel, wrung it out, and laid it on my forehead. "I'm
sorry, Angela. That was a bad scene for you to witness."

"What happened?" I asked.

"Nothing. It's all over." Uncle Al's voice was muf-
fled as he held a handkerchief to his bleeding lip. "The
Wroboskis are kaput. The *Weasel* has joined the *chickens*."

I noticed the gun lying on the table, and it gave me a cold, edgy feeling as if a ghost were in the room. Dad followed my look and reached to push the gun away, but Uncle Al quickly snatched it.

"Just tell me one thing, Weasel," Uncle Al said as he stuck the gun beneath his coat. "Why'd you run?"

Dad glanced at the floor.

"What happened, Weasel?" Uncle Al's voice was regaining its power. "You had it all planned out, even on a computer."

He didn't seem to care that I was there listening, but I barely heard them, anyway. I must have been in shock.

"*Why*, after all our planning, did I have to do the job myself? I'm not the *front-runner* of these operations — I'm the *brains*!"

Dad remained silent.

"So where did you go?"

"To the café."

"To the café?"

"I walked over to the New Day Café and bought a burger to get an alibi. Saw some guys I knew in there. They'll vouch for me."

"With that black coat on that I lent you, and shades, you leave the balaclava in the car and take off for a burger on a Friday morning? A Catholic isn't even supposed to *eat* meat on Fridays!"

It seemed a weird time to bring in religion, but I guess an alibi had to be tight. Theirs was anything but.

"Well, I had money!" Dad protested.

Like Felix the Cat, my eyes shifted from Uncle Al to Dad and back again. Both faces were stony, stubborn, and resentful.

A knock sounded on the front door. Uncle Al was out of his chair and through the back door quick as a racehorse from the starting gate.

Dad peered through the curtain. "It's that artsy woman!" he whispered hoarsely.

I couldn't believe it. There stood Mrs. Singer, Hannah's mother, peering through the screen.

"Good morning, Angela!" she said brightly. "I hope I'm not disturbing anything. Would this be a good time to view your father's artwork?"

I was speechless.

Dad heard and came to the door. He was deathly white, but more in control than usual. "I'm sorry, Julia. I think I've got the flu. Angela, can you get down some of my sketches?"

"Sure."

I reached up, robot-like, and removed some taped pictures from the wall around the computer area. Dad gave me a bag, and I stuck them inside, along with some other ones from the trunk. Mrs. Singer thanked him and turned to go.

"I hope you feel better soon, Nick," she said. "Hot lemon and Aspirin!" Then she added, "Oh, I hear you've arranged for some private tutoring! When I return these, I'll bring you some of the boys' books that might help. Education is certainly a step in the right direction. Good luck!" She waved cheerily and returned to her car, just as Mom strode up the walk.

I stood with my back against the closed door, hardly daring to breathe, while Dad hurriedly filled Mom in. She was pretty calm, considering.

I'd never before heard such a sure tone in Dad's voice. "Then that art lady, Julia, came. Boy, did Al run!"

"Julia?" is all she said.

He grinned lopsidedly. "We got talking at Sports Day. Artists don't call each other mister and missus. Come on, I'll make some tea. We're all pretty shook."

No kidding.

When Uncle Al saw that the coast was clear, he edged back into the kitchen. He was nervous, and for good reason. To them Mom was scarier than a judge.

"I gotta blow this joint," he said. "The whole place is gonna be lousy with cops. Armed robbery!" He gave Dad a disgusted look, which came off more funny than sinister with his swollen lip. In fact, Uncle Al seemed to have lost his fierceness.

"It was you or me," Dad said quietly. "If I'd gone in there to rob that bank machine the way we planned, I would have gotten caught. I'd be just like Burt Lancaster."

Uncle Al squinted. "Huh?"

"Burt Lancaster in that movie, *Bird Man of Alcatraz*. Burt's sitting there in jail with nothing to do. He thinks about his mother, and that woman who wants to marry him. But he's not part of their scene no more. So he goes off by himself and raises canaries."

We looked over at Patsy, who was strangely quiet following his recent burst of song.

"*I'll* be raising those things now," Uncle Al said. He turned to head out the back door. "So long, bird brain — and bird brain's kid."

"Hey, just a minute!" Dad followed him to the door. "You told me if I got some dough together, you'd let me buy my own cab and drive for Dial-a-Dream. Buy into the business. You said just this one job would get me the cash ..."

"Yeah, and you turned cold! Deal's off!"

"Deal's *on*," Dad said. "You owe me, from all those other jobs. You set me up as the patsy — I did time twice on account of you! And I didn't sing. So you owe me big time."

Dad and Uncle Al glared at each other.

"Who's gonna run Dial-a-Dream while you're hiding out?" Dad demanded. "You're hotter than a two-dollar pistol! You'll have to cool off in Mexico or someplace."

"Good idea," Uncle Al said.

"I've been learning computers, Connie can do book-keeping and have a car to drive, and Angela can keep the place tidy and answer phones after school and on week-ends when most of the calls come in," Dad said. "We'll run the business for you."

"No chance. You've got to have my signature to do that, and I'm not giving it."

"Yes, you are," I said. Mom and I pushed a piece of a paper at him. "You can sign right here that Dad's part owner and manager of Dial-a-Dream. Or I'll send you a yellow canary."

"You'd what!" Uncle Al said as he and Dad turned shocked faces toward me.

"My dad has a jail record because you made him your patsy," I said to Uncle Al. "So you owe him, just like he says."

"Sign!" Mom demanded.

There was a bang outside. We all jumped, but though it was only a car backfiring, it was enough to make Uncle Al seize the pen and scrawl his signature, "Alvin Wroboski," under where I'd written the date, and "Nick Wroboski is manager of Dial-a-Dream until I return."

Uncle Al stuck out his hand to Dad. "Never thought I'd shake the paw of a weasel, but I worked too hard to let the business go. And there's no one else to carry on." He glowered at Mom and me. Then he tossed the Caddy keys to her. "Here, Con, in memory of the good old days."

She caught them. "Thanks, and here's to some good *new* days." Oddly, she smiled at Uncle Al, a brilliant wide grin.

He nodded curtly, and then he was gone.

22
Fugitive!

Newspaper headlines the next day said it all: BANK EMPLOYEE WOUNDED IN LINE OF DUTY, and in smaller letters FUGITIVE STILL AT LARGE. I was afraid to read the article, but of course I did, feeling like Gemma who read detective magazines to look for relatives' names. But unlike Gemma, I was hoping I didn't see any.

A holdup at First Trust on Seventh Street and Fourth Avenue yesterday has sent one man to hospital with a bullet wound to his leg and netted a loss of over $10,000 to the bank.

A man, posing as a customer, followed one of the young bank clerks into the room located behind a wall of bank machines. Once inside, the bandit slipped on a balaclava, locked the door, and told the employee to keep quiet and do as he was told.

"I felt a gun at my back!" said the shaken employee. "It was poking right between my shoulder blades."

He was then ordered to open a metal suitcase he was carrying, which was filled with cash to replenish the bank machine money bins.

The employee complied, "shaking like a leaf."

Wow! I scanned the article quickly, hoping my dad or Uncle Al weren't mentioned.

The newspaper said the robber stuffed the money into a black leather briefcase. Noticing a wall-mounted video camera in a metal casing, and thinking it had recorded the action, he fired a shot at it. The bullet ricocheted off the camera and a granite wall and hit the bank clerk in the leg. From his hospital bed the employee said he was lucky to be alive.

A full-scale search was underway for the robber. No suspects. He had his face covered, and witnesses' descriptions differed, but police would be questioning local people known to have criminal records.

"They're on a canary hunt for singers," Dad said disgustedly. "Well, they won't find one here — except for that thing." He pointed an accusing finger at Patsy. "Angel, you've seen nothing. You've heard nothing."

"Right."

"It's family business."

"Right."

So far Uncle Al was in the clear. The newspaper added that the suspect could also be the person responsible for ripping off bank machines throughout the city over the past couple of months. Since June. Since Dad's arrival home.

The scam was called bank-machine stuffing, with the culprit covering the cash-dispensing slot with a metal plate so a customer's money would get stuck. When he left, the criminal would go in, remove the plate, and snatch out the money. The security cameras had fuzzy images, but it looked more like a woman than a man, so it couldn't have been Dad. That was a relief, but I didn't want to think about it anymore. The suspect had blond frizzy hair and wore fancy dark sunglasses.

When the police arrived at our house, we were drinking tea like a normal family. They asked Dad to come out to the car with them for some questions. He returned in fifteen minutes and gave us a thumbs-up sign. "No one here is going to 'sing' except that little squawker," Dad said, gesturing at Patsy. Family business.

The next day Dad and I walked downtown to the Dial-a-Dream office. The Cadillac was parked behind the office building. We entered the office, with Dad using his handy-dandy door opener.

I couldn't believe the shape the office was in. My image of Uncle Al as a rich businessman crashed pretty fast. Bundles of receipts had been carelessly thrown into shoeboxes, and handwritten invoices into others. The desk was a mess of unopened letters and bills and overflowing ashtrays. Dozens of voice-mail messages waited unanswered.

"Okay, where do we start?" Dad asked.

"Do what Uncle Al would when he gets in a fix — hire a lawyer!" I said.

"Good idea."

It took us several weeks to sort stuff out, including having Dad's name registered as manager. We convinced him to hire a real accountant, who discovered that Uncle Al, like his hero, Al Capone, had never paid taxes, or many other bills. In short, the place was a mess, with the phone ringing constantly with people wanting service.

"Ryan, we need you to help set up Uncle Al's computer," I said.

Then I made another phone call. "Hannah, remember you said we could install some computer programs that you have? Well, I need them. Can you bring them to the Dial-a-Dream office?" I gave her the address, ignoring her questions. "I'll tell you all about it when you get here," I said, and hung up.

It was Gemma, though, who offered real help. "Hey, how about hiring me part-time as the driver?" she asked Dad.

"On one condition," Dad said. "You dump Jerry."

He and Gemma stared at each other. "Yeah, sure. I was thinking of it, anyway. He's a loser."

So the Wroboskis were in business! And as Uncle Al once said, "It's even legal, Your Honour!"

Hannah came down with the program discs, and Ryan installed them. Then we went over to the New Day Café to have a real good talk.

"Angela, I'm sorry, but I have to ask. Do you think your family knows anything about that robbery at our bank? Or stealing from the ATMs?"

"*Your* bank?" I said. I could barely breathe.

"*Your* bank, that your dad runs," Ryan said.

"Yes, the bank that my dad's manager of. Didn't you know? You must've heard it on the radio or TV or in the papers. It's big news."

I sipped my Coke. This was tough. Hannah's dad's bank!

Truth or lies? I recalled Dad's words when Mom brought my canary home for my fifteenth birthday: *A canary is a sign of a squealer. That's the lowest form of life. And a patsy's a fall guy, someone set up to take the rap.*

I glanced across the table at Hannah and Ryan. What would they do if they knew the truth? Would Ryan help us anymore? Would Hannah go to her father? Their parents would all freak, just as I was now. The police would come, maybe charge Dad with being an accomplice, even though he didn't actually do the crime. Might Gemma be a suspect in the machine-stuffing thing, or charged with knowing about the bank robbery? All these problems just as everyone had the opportunity of a lifetime? It would ruin forever our chances for success. Truth or dare? What were more important — friends or family? I needed both!

"I don't know anything about this bank robbery or the ATM stuff except what I've read in the paper," I said, amazed at how calm my voice sounded. "And I'm sure my mom and dad don't, either. You can't go around accusing people of things like that, you know. In this

162

country a person is innocent until proven guilty. And it's the courts that decide, not kids."

"I'm sorry," Hannah said. "I feel awful about this whole thing. I just thought ... oh, never mind. Can we just forget it?"

"Sure. Uh, how is the guy who got shot?"

"He's fine. The bullet just grazed his leg. He'll be back at work next week."

"Good. Well, I've got to go, now. I'll leave you two here to discuss — computers! I have a business to run." I laughed, and they laughed a little, too.

"By the way," Hannah said, "Mom thinks your dad's artwork is quite brilliant. She's teaching a still life art class in September and wants to hire him to give talks and workshops. Think he'd be interested?"

"He probably would," I said. "Have her call him — at his office."

Wow! That sounded good. I was going to ask Mom to buy Dad a briefcase.

23
Dial-a-Dream

At lunchtime on Saturday Mom and I were thinking of walking down to the Dial-a-Dream office to take Dad a sandwich when we heard a car pull up. We looked out through the open door. It was Gemma and Grandma, driving up in the big black Caddy.

"My baby!" Grandma *oomphed* out of the leather seat and held out her arms to me. I became instantly smothered in a bear hug, but this bear smelled of perfume, which she got as samples from Gemma. Then she opened her arms to scoop Mom inside, too, and we were squashed against her big bosom.

"I brought you something," Grandma said as she released us. She fumbled in her shopping bag and came out with black T-shirts with DIAL-A-DREAM printed across the front in bright pink neon letters. "You girls wear them all over town. Be good advertising. We gotta be proud of our business."

"Our business?" I said with a smile.

"Yes, *our* business! Al never finished paying me for the car, so the lawyer says I own it. How do you like that?"

We pulled on the T-shirts, laughing as we took turns in front of the mirror to admire our new uniforms.

"I never did have much use for Al," Grandma continued, "but he's family, and I can't wish ill of him. Now he's gone on some big holiday and given us the business to run, and a Cadillac car. No, I can't hold a grudge."

"Coffee's ready," Mom said, setting out four mugs.

"Maybe he's down in Toronto working the horseracing track like Nick did," Gemma suggested.

"Poor Nicky," Grandma said. "I remember that trip. He went down there like a big shot on an airplane and everything. Got arrested. They brought him back like cargo."

"That's past," I said. "Dad's a businessman now."

"It's funny that Al would leave town so quickly," Grandma said. "I wonder if he had anything to do with that bank robbery?"

"I told him to get a bank loan, but I didn't think he'd take me that seriously!" Gemma slapped me on the shoulder, urging me to get the joke.

"Here, Mamma, drink your coffee," Mom said.

Grandma leaned forward in her chair and sipped the coffee. "I'm gonna pray to St. Jude for your Uncle Al, wherever he is, same as I did for your daddy. That's the saint for hopeless cases. He sure heard my prayers for Nicky."

"We could all use a little help from above," Mom said thoughtfully, and I agreed.

"Nicky was always delicate, while Al was the strong one," Grandma continued. "Now we don't know where Al is, and Nicky's gonna be a businessman. Such a strange world."

"Where are Nick's pictures?" Gemma asked, noticing blank places on the wall. The only ones left were family portraits: Mom clutching the bouquet of daisies; me wearing a big straw hat and holding Patsy up on my finger; Gemma and Grandma at the kitchen table, peeling potatoes and laughing; Grandpa Hank with Trixie in their garden; Uncle Al looking like a millionaire, leaning against the shiny black Dial-a-Dream Caddy.

But the other pictures, Gemma's favourites, were gone.

"They're over at my friend Hannah Singer's place," I said. "Her mom came here to see Dad's work, and he loaned them to her. They're both artists, you know. Mrs. Singer wants him to give lectures to her art class this fall."

"That *bank manager* Singer?" Gemma asked, incredulous. "The paper said it was his bank that was hit."

I felt my face flush. "Yeah, could be."

Gemma started laughing. Then I did, too, thinking of Mr. and Mrs. Singer examining Dad's art: *Dead Oak Tree with Noose, Two Little Ghouls in Blue, Scarface's Valentine*, sketches of Dad's fellow cons, a detailed layout of the warden's office.

Mom and I walked Grandma and Gemma out to the car. I ran my hand along the shiny black fender of our Cadillac. The words DIAL-A-DREAM glowed brightly in the noonday sun, reflecting off the polished paint.

Perhaps our family would never be television models of perfection, but they were my flesh and blood. And they were trying hard. I was becoming prouder of them every day, especially Dad because he had the farthest to travel along the road to respectability, pulling Gemma — and maybe even someday Uncle Al — along with him. We'd be okay. Our family being together, with a future, was our shared dream. We were all front-runners now.

Also by
Shirlee Smith Matheson

The Gambler's Daughter
978-1-55002-718-1
$11.99

In early 1940s British Columbia, teen-age Loretta, younger brother Teddy, and their gambling stepfather, "Bean Trap" Braden, are one step ahead of the law and a band of angry miners. Run out of town for winning more than his share of the miners' wages, Bean Trap and the children jump borders, hide out in ghost towns, and stow away on trucks, sleds, and trains. Now Loretta must take the biggest gamble of all. Can she and Teddy get out of the game and start a new life, or are the stakes too high?

Available at your favourite bookseller.